Camp Fossil Eyes

Digging for the Origins of Words

Mark Abley

illustrated by Kathryn Adams

annick press
toronto + new york + vancouver

Annick Press Ltd.

Edited by Pam Robertson
Copyedited by Geri Rowlatt
Proofread by Tanya Trafford
Cover and interior design by Black Eye Design
Cover and interior illustrations by Kathryn Adams

We acknowledge the support of the Canada Council for the Arts, the Ontario Arts Council, and the Government of Canada through the Book Publishing Industry Development Program (BPIDP) for our publishing activities.

Cataloging in Publication

Abley, Mark, 1955-
    Camp Fossil Eyes : digging for the origins of words / by Mark Abley ; illustrated by Kathryn Adams.

Includes bibliographical references and index.
ISBN 978-1-55451-181-5 (bound).—ISBN 978-1-55451-180-8 (pbk.)

    1. English language—Etymology—Juvenile fiction. 2. English language—Etymology—Juvenile literature.
I. Adams, Kathryn II. Title.
PS8551.B45 C35 2009   jC813'.54   C2009-901207-3

Printed and bound in China

Published in the U.S.A. by **Distributed in Canada by** **Distributed in the U.S.A. by**
Annick Press (U.S.) Ltd.   Firefly Books Ltd.   Firefly Books (U.S.) Inc.
                              66 Leek Crescent   P.O. Box 1338
                              Richmond Hill, ON   Ellicott Station
                              L4B 1H1   Buffalo, NY 14205

Visit our website at www.annickpress.com

To Julie and Craig Hartley,
the founding directors of Centauri Arts Camp,
which is even more fun (and much safer) than Camp Fossil Eyes

Where did our language come from?

Indigenous Languages   10–21

Recent Words   23–29

Old English   35–47

French   50–58

Old Norse   63–68

Dutch   72–75

Latin   76–83

Persian   84–85

Spanish   86–89

Greek   90–99

Proto-Indo-European   100–109

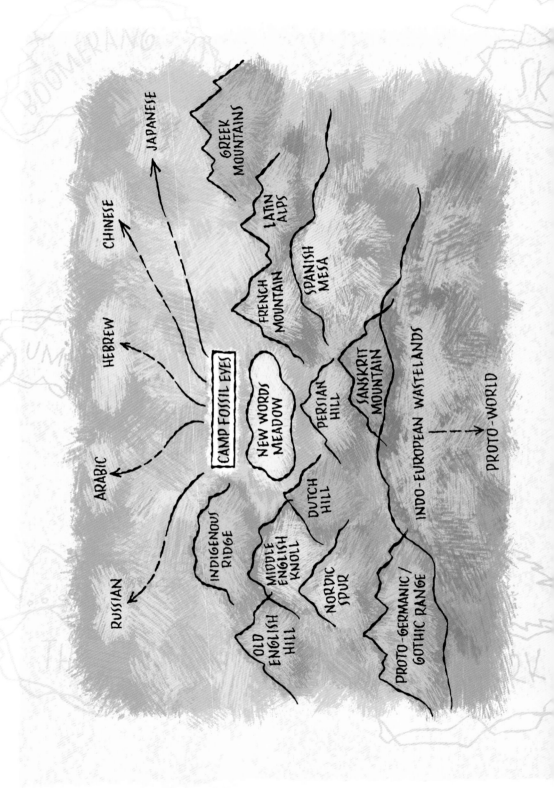

To: parents
From: Jillian Boswell
Sent: July 5
Subject: Middle of Nowhere

· ·

Dear Mother and Father,

My counselor says I have to write you a letter. I'm supposed to tell you how wonderful life is at Camp Fossil Eyes.

I don't think it's wonderful at all. I know you're moving across the continent and starting new jobs this month, and you made it depressingly clear you want Alex and me out of the way. But why did you have to send us to a dead zone like this?

The flight was long and boring. After we staggered off the plane, we were forced to sit squashed up in the back of a dusty old van all the

way to camp. The
last part of the trip
was over a bumpy
gravel road—it was
so not fun. When we
finally scrambled out,
we were somewhere
in the middle of these
bare, rocky hills that
my counselor calls the
badlands. She says we'll
find out the reason soon,
but it's obvious to me:

Everything is bad here.
The wind howls, the nights are cold, and even the few plants look
sort of gray. There are no malls, no movie theaters, no coffee shops,
not even any stores—it's a nightmare place to be wasting most of a
month.

I suppose I should tell you that my little brother seems to be okay
with it. But I would respectfully ask you to send me a plane ticket
home, whatever "home" means now.

Annoyed,

Jillian

To: Dad & Mom
From: Alex Boswell
Sent: July 6
Subject: Fossils

. . . .

Dear Mom and Dad,

This is the weirdest place. Jill is sulking over on the girls' side of camp and I'm still trying to figure it all out. The food seems to be pretty good, the night sky is spectacular, and I'm getting on okay with the

three other guys in my cabin. They're my age, though one of them will be turning 14 next month. Noah, my counselor, is a tall guy with sideburns and glasses, and he has this habit of scratching his ears till they turn red. When I asked what he did when he wasn't at camp, he said, "I'm training to be an etymologist."

"A *what*?" I said.

It turns out that etymologists are people who check into the origins of words. Basically, they decide where language comes from. Noah said that after we get familiar with the area and complete some outdoor training, that's what we'll be doing this summer: hunting for words and learning where they began. It's kind of neat to have a counselor who's more of a nerd than I am.

"My mom promised me we'd go fossil hunting," I told him.

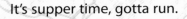

"Oh, you will," he said, with a weird kind of laugh, "you will. Don't worry."

I don't get it. Fossils are ancient bones, right? How can a word be a fossil?

It's supper time, gotta run.

Bye for now,

Alex

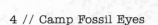

To: parents
From: Jillian Boswell
Sent: July 7
Subject: Get me out of here

. . . .

Mother, Father,

I need to leave.

Now.

Of all the ridiculous places you have forced me to visit, including that lame historical camp when I was still recovering from Grade 5, this is the worst. The cabins verge on the primitive and the showers are pathetic. Except for the occasional computer access, I feel like I'm living in the Middle Ages. My counselor is a redhead named Kelly who is so gung-ho about everything here, I can't stand it. At lunch, she stood up with a huge grin and announced that tomorrow she intends to lead us across these naked, ugly hills on "an exciting hunt for indigenous words."

I haven't washed my hair in like four days and now I'm supposed to go on a major hike? And what in the world is word hunting?

I'll probably get bitten by an indigenous rattlesnake or attacked by an indigenous coyote or something. Anyway, don't people hunt for words in dictionaries?

Alexander appears to be happy. I am not.

I need to leave. *Now*.

Jillian

To: Dad & Mom
From: Alex Boswell
Sent: July 8
Subject: Chipmunks

. . . .

Dear Mom and Dad,

I'm lying on my bunk after dinner, with the wind whipping up dust devils outside our cabin. It's been the most incredible day. I did so much hiking and learned so much stuff, I hardly know where to start!

After breakfast, we all gathered in the common area outside to listen to the camp director, Dr. Murray. He's a gray-haired man with twinkly eyes and a long beard that must get itchy in the heat. He said now that we were familiar with the daily routine, it was time we discovered what this camp is all about. He asked if anybody could guess why it has the name "Fossil Eyes."

Daniel, this guy in my cabin, put up his hand and said it was because we had to keep our eyes open for dinosaur bones. That wasn't right. Amina, who's been trying to make friends with Jill, thought it was because if we did come across any fossils, eyes were the best type to find. That wasn't right either. There was a long silence, and Dr. Murray was looking at us all with a sad expression, so I stuck my hand in the air and said, "Because fossils help you see things, like the past?"

Dr. Murray smiled because that was the right answer, or part of it. He said whenever he left his desk and walked through the camp, he remembered some lines written by an American author named

Ralph Waldo Emerson. I can tell you the exact words because Dr. Murray gave everyone a piece of fancy paper with the quotation on it and asked us to keep it safe in our binders: "The etymologist finds the deadest word to have been once a brilliant picture. Language is fossil poetry."

So that's the idea behind Camp Fossil Eyes—it's a place to study the fossils of words. Dr. Murray said that here in these badlands, words take on a physical shape. No one knows why, but it seems to be the only place in the world where this happens. If you knew where to look, and if you were patient enough, you could eventually discover hundreds of thousands of different words. Sometimes we'll have to dig, but in many cases the fossils will be near the surface—the newer words should be in plain view.

Dr. Murray explained that a lot of words came into our language from other sources— languages that have been around for many centuries—and over the next few weeks, we'll concentrate our fossil hunting on particular ridges, hills, and mountains: one for French, one for Ancient Greek, and so on. And the coolest part is that the badlands act like a mirror showing the evolution of English. The languages that gave us the most words are also the ones that have the biggest geographical formations.

Most of us were still looking kind of stunned—what a bizarre place!—when Dr. Murray asked us to form into groups of about six or eight kids, each group with a counselor. The counselors gave us water bottles and apples and tiny metal spades to put in our backpacks. Then we set off for Indigenous Ridge. Well, most of us did. Jill wanted to stay behind. She's still being difficult, as you would say, Mom.

Noah turned out to be a better climber than I expected. He must have great leg muscles—he got to the top of the high ridge faster than any of the campers. The view was awesome—grassy hills with some steep valleys in between that seem to go on forever.

When we'd joined him at the top—this guy called Steven was sweating like crazy—Noah said that today we'd be searching for indigenous words. Most of us didn't understand what he meant, so he explained: they're words that come from a language that belongs to the first people in an area.

"You mean like the native Indians?" I asked.

"That's right," he answered. "They're indigenous to North America. If we look carefully, I'm sure we'll find a few of their words today. But there are other indigenous peoples all over the world."

So we started poking around. At first we didn't find anything, just dirt and scrubby grass and the odd cactus. My back started to ache from all the bending. Then I heard Steven give a shout.

"Over here!" he called. "There's something sticking up!"

We hustled over to the patch of hillside where he was standing. And sure enough, a sharp little rock was poking out of the dirt. Noah took his spade out of his backpack and showed us how to excavate carefully around the rock, taking care not to damage the fossil itself. Then he and Steven gently pulled the fossil from the ground and held it up to the light.

"It's **chipmunk**," Noah said as he smoothed it off. "If you hold the stone up to the light, you'll be able to see some faint marks on it. The word has a history—every word has a history. This word comes from the Ojibwa of Canada's northern forests. They called it *ajidamoo*, which means 'an animal who goes down trees upside down.'"

"How can you get all that in a single word?" a girl asked.

"Well," Noah said, "we know that *ajid* means 'upside down' in Ojibwa. So maybe the literal meaning is more like upside-down traveling animal. We could find out because Ojibwa is still spoken by tens of thousands of people today." He paused and turned the fossil over in his hands. "People changed the way the word is pronounced when they started using it in English. They shortened the number of syllables and added a few consonants at the end. Back in the 19th century, they wrote it down as 'a chitmunk.' Later it became a chipmunk. It can take a long while before a word ends up with a spelling everyone uses."

I could see that Steven was feeling proud of himself. "Do I get to keep it?" he asked, reaching for the fossil.

"I'm sorry," Noah said. "We're not allowed to carry the fossils away with us. They have to stay on the ridge, because they belong to everyone. But now that Steven has found one, why don't the rest of you see if you can match him?"

Pretty soon it seemed like the whole of Indigenous Ridge—oops, I gotta sign off, it's Daniel's turn on the computer. I'll try to finish this message later…

To: Dad & Mom
From: Alex Boswell
Sent: July 8
Subject: Buccaneers

. . . .

Hi again,

I'm back. I figure I've got another 25 minutes before lights out. Don't be surprised if I write a lot this month—I plan to read through the Sent Messages folder when I get home, and it'll become the diary I'm not keeping.

Like I was saying, after Steven found the first fossil on Indigenous Ridge, we realized that the hillside was full of them. Noah said that for the most interesting ones, he'd give us notes that we could put in our binders. And after hunting for a while, I found a really crazy fossil. The sun was burning down, and I was starting to get discouraged because it seemed like the fossils were avoiding me. Then I noticed this strange-looking rock on a sandy slope above me. I climbed up to it and started digging and tugging and pushing away the sand.

Finally it came free. I hauled it over to Noah, and he was so happy that he called everyone else over to see.

"Alex has discovered **buccaneer**," he said. "It's got an astonishing history." It looked to me like the fossil had several different kinds of writing on it, one on top of another. Noah explained why: the fossil embodies the word's history. All the stuff that happened to it over time—changes in meaning, changes in spelling and pronunciation, the way it moved from one language to another—appears on the rock's surface and affects its shape.

When we got back to camp Noah wrote out the details of buccaneer for me. The word came into English a few hundred years ago from the French, who spelled it *boucanier*. The *boucaniers* were outlaw guys on a couple of islands in the Caribbean who would hunt wild pigs and steal cows and then smoke the meat on a wooden frame they called a *boucan*. They sold the meat to sailors on passing ships. So before they turned into pirates, buccaneers were plain old barbecuers. Eventually, they figured out they could get more gold by raiding the ships than by feeding the sailors.

But a *boucan* wasn't a word that anybody in France would have known, because originally it belonged to the Tupí Indians on the coast of Brazil. The Portuguese were the first Europeans to invade Brazil, and they must have noticed that the Tupí used a frame to cook their meat. The Tupí called the frame a *mocaém*, or maybe a *bocaém*, and the Portuguese borrowed their word and passed it on to the French as *boucan*. So the fossil I found today has got an English layer, a French layer, a Portuguese layer, and, oldest of all, a Tupí layer. Cool, huh?

Later in the afternoon I found the fossil for **sockeye**. Noah said it was *su-key*, meaning "red fish," in the language of some of the Salish Indians who

still live in the Pacific Northwest. I used to wonder why a creature with no feet would be named after socks. Now I know: it's just an accident of spelling.

Most of us found at least one fossil today, but there's this girl called Keshia who's got an amazing talent for it. She must have discovered six, maybe seven. Two of her words, **hurricane** and **hammock**, reached us from a people who are totally extinct. They belonged to the Taino, an indigenous group in the Caribbean who died out after the Europeans got there— they had no guns and couldn't cope with foreign diseases. But we still use a few of their words! Keshia said this made her feel spooked.

"Language has a memory," Noah told her, "but not a conscience." I guess she must have looked blank because he added that words are a great way of remembering and honoring people who are no longer around—although words can never put the past right. Luckily, Keshia also found the fossil for **chocolate**: *xocolatl*, or "bitter water" to the Nahuatl people of Mexico. And they're still very much alive.

It was a long hike back so I'm tired. But if every day is going to be like today, this'll be an awesome summer. Thank you for finding out about this place!

Lots of love,

Alex

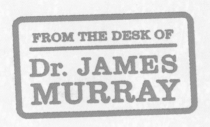
Two words from indigenous languages

squash

Sometimes words that are spelled the same and sound the same have completely different meanings and origins. **Squash** is a good example. As a verb, meaning "to crush something," it's an English

version of an old French word, *esquasser*. As a noun, squash can refer to a game you play on an indoor court with a ball and racquets, a game that was invented in the 1880s. But as another noun—the name for the vegetable that fed many of North America's indigenous peoples—squash has been around since 1643.

Early colonists in America didn't recognize the vegetable because nothing quite like it grew in Britain. They gathered the food—and the word—from the original residents of New England. The word as we know it is short for *askutasquash*, which meant "eaten raw" in the language of the Narragansett. They belonged to the Algonquian family of peoples, along with larger and better-known groups like the Cree, Mi'kmaq, and Ojibwa. Most of the Narragansett lived in what's now the state of Rhode Island. A few thousand of them are still around, but their language died out centuries ago.

And, of course, most people today prefer to eat their squash cooked.

As settlers muscled onto Narragansett lands, they learned many new words and adapted them for their own purposes. **Papoose** (an infant or small child) and **quahog** (a hard-shelled clam) both come from Narragansett. Other Algonquian languages gave us the names of well-known animals (**raccoon**, **skunk**, **caribou**, **moose**), plants (**pecan**, **persimmon**, **hickory**), and objects (**moccasin**, **toboggan**). In most of these cases, the English word is shorter than the original one. Hickory, for example, was originally *pocohiquara*.

Apart from these words, the Algonquian languages also gave us some of the most famous place-names in

North America. The city of **Chicago**, the lake and state of **Michigan**, and the river and state of **Mississippi** are examples. Some people say that Chicago was taken from an Algonquian word for "wild leek" or "wild onion field," but others believe the name originally meant "skunk land"—or just "skunk."

boomerang

When European settlers first arrived in Australia in the late 18th century, they were dumbfounded by what seemed to them a very peculiar landscape. It was home to an equally peculiar assortment of animals and plants. There were big mammals that hopped, big birds that couldn't fly, and small mammals that laid eggs. The settlers were also baffled by the many aboriginal peoples, who spoke more than 300 languages. To the Aboriginals, of course, the land, animals, and

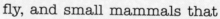

plants were normal, and the pale-skinned newcomers were the peculiar ones.

Most of the indigenous Australian words that entered the English language didn't change much from their original form. They refer to particular animals (**kangaroo**, **wombat**) or to features in the natural environment (a **billabong** is a water hole; a **willy-willy** is a dust devil or whirlwind). But it's thanks to the inventiveness of the aboriginal peoples that we have the word **boomerang**—a curved piece of hardwood that can return to the thrower. Today, children often play with boomerangs; centuries ago, they were not toys but weapons.

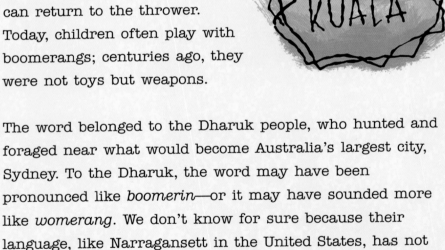

The word belonged to the Dharuk people, who hunted and foraged near what would become Australia's largest city, Sydney. To the Dharuk, the word may have been pronounced like *boomerin*—or it may have sounded more like *womerang*. We don't know for sure because their language, like Narragansett in the United States, has not survived. Apart from boomerang, the Dharuk language also gave us **dingo** and **koala**.

Over the course of time, words sometimes take on an extra sense besides their original meaning. They grow to suggest a feeling or an idea, not just a physical object. We call this a "metaphorical meaning." Suppose that a girl spreads an unpleasant story about a classmate—but her friends quickly discover that it's a lie. The girl who made up the tale is now in big trouble. We can say that the story has boomeranged on her: it has come back to hurt her. That kind of damage, which has nothing to do with Australian throwing sticks, is the metaphorical meaning of boomerang.

To: parents
cc: Kelly Monahan
From: Jillian Boswell
Sent: July 9
Subject: Fun

. . . .

Dear parental people,

My demon counselor says I have to write and tell you what fun we had today.

We had fun today.

Jillian

p.s. Meh.

To: Karen and Michael Boswell

From: Kelly Monahan

Sent: July 9

Subject: Your daughter

. . . .

Dear Mr. and Mrs. Boswell,

This is Jill's counselor, Kelly. Don't worry, nothing terrible has happened. I think Jill has really started to enjoy herself in the last day or two. But she doesn't want to admit it. My hunch is that she's trying to punish you for moving and taking her away from her home and her old friends. Maybe she also thinks she might appear uncool if she let herself have fun like everybody else.

I realize you might be worrying about her. And when she copied me on her very brief message earlier this evening, I decided I should take a few minutes to tell you what we did today.

As you know, this is a camp where young people discover the fun of word origins and the joy of language. Jill decided she wasn't ready to go on a long hike this morning, so she didn't accompany her brother and most of the other kids up to Indigenous Ridge, as we call it here. Instead, she and two other 15-year-old girls stayed with me, close to home. We strolled over to a nearby meadow full of pebbles and tiny wildflowers. They all thought we were just out for an easy hike, but I surprised them. Together, we began to look for words that were born in the 20th century or the early 21st—they're still so new, you can find them right at the surface. I wanted the girls to know that even young and familiar words can have a surprising story.

In a patch of loose gravel, Jill's friend Amina discovered the fossil for **dadrock,** a recently created word meaning "music played by middle-aged rockers." Jill said she uses the word occasionally at home (sorry, Mr. Boswell). The girls were astounded when I told them that **rock**, used as a verb, goes back 1,000 years or more to the Old English word *roccian*, meaning "to sway," and that **dad** has been around for a good 500 years, maybe longer. But only in the past few years did people stick these two old words together to create something new.

I happened to be searching close to Jill when she noticed the fossil for **hipster** amid the forget-me-nots. She let out a yelp and picked it up gently. In general, as Jill knew, it now refers to people who define themselves as cool, who love the arts, who dress stylishly but shop at thrift stores, who listen to indie music, and so on. Yet the word has a complicated history: I told her that back in the 1940s, it meant someone who was "hip," or smart and well-informed. Eventually, people in the San Francisco area started talking about **hippies** instead of hipsters—and that might have happened because of *another* use of hipster: pants that ride low on the hips, or **hip-huggers**. Then hippies came to mean one group of young people—or maybe not so young—and hipsters came to mean another. Sometimes when you're trying to trace a word's origin, one usage gets in the way of another. I have to admit Jill was looking a little dazed at this point.

As I told her and the other girls, hipster is one of those words that has no simple definition because it means something a little different to everyone who thinks about it. Of course, many words come with a single, obvious meaning, like **antelope** or **acne**. You can't say an antelope is a politician; you can't say that acne is a breakfast cereal. But lots of other words, like hipster, keep on changing. Occasionally people even fight over the meaning. And dictionaries aren't always much help.

After that, Jill did great. She found a few other words as well, and when we got back to camp I was able to give her detailed notes on them to insert in her binder. We had some issues in the first few days she was here, but now she's doing fine.

Best wishes,

Kelly Monahan

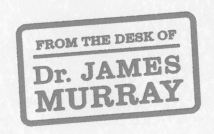
Two recent words

podcast

This word was
invented in the
early years of
the 21ˢᵗ century.
It means a
delivery of audio
files over the
Internet, usually

downloaded onto an iPod or MP3 player so that the
subscriber can listen to the file anywhere. A new idea, a
new word—but its roots are old.

The term **pod** goes all the way back to the 17ᵗʰ century,
and it means a small case that holds peas, beans, or
insect eggs. Arthur C. Clarke, an author of many science-
fiction novels and screenplays, picked up the term when
he wrote the script for the classic 1968 movie *2001:
A Space Odyssey.* Imagining a spacecraft that could take
astronauts (and a talking computer named HAL) all
the way to Jupiter, Clarke conceived of a one-person

maintenance vehicle called the EVA Pod. In turn, an advertising copywriter named Vinnie Chieco remembered the EVA Pod when Apple Inc. asked him to come up with a name for a new audio device in 2001. Inspired by *2001*, Chieco suggested "iPod."

"Cast," the second half of the word, is taken from **broadcast**—but broadcasting did not always refer to sounds or images. The term sprang to life in England around 1760, long before radios, TV sets, and audio players had been invented. It was an agricultural word for the scattering of seed. The common link between the two meanings is the idea of broad transmission across the land—first of seeds, then of sounds.

Because it combines two elements— "pod" and "cast"—**podcast** is a classic example of what linguists call a portmanteau word. Other portmanteau words include **brunch** (which mixes the first two letters of "breakfast" with the last four of "lunch") and **smog** (a blend of "smoke" and "fog").

meh

In "Hungry Hungry Homer," an episode of *The Simpsons*, Homer asks his two older children if they'd like to go visit the Blockoland theme park. Bart and Lisa reply in unison, "Meh!" Homer tries again: "But the TV gave the impression..." "We said 'meh,'" Bart interrupts. "*M-E-H*," adds Lisa. "Meh."

Meh means boring, it means whatever, it means who cares? And while Lisa and Bart made it wildly popular, it's possible this brief bleat goes back a lot further in time. Some etymologists believe its source is in Yiddish—the main language of Europe's Jews until most of their communities were destroyed in the Holocaust. One earlier episode of *The Simpsons* had also featured meh, or a dismissive noise very like it.

Until Lisa spelled out the word, it remained obscure. But then, all of a sudden, it became a mainstay of pop culture. Soon a journalist could write, "Ryan Opray got voted off *Survivor*. Meh." A newspaper columnist summed up a movie with the words, "It's kind of meh, but the cast is awesome." Everyone from political observers to sports commentators grabbed hold of the word and ran with it.

Meh may not flourish for long. We can't tell. Not all the new expressions that emerge from TV shows will remain in the language; people living in 2100 may look back on meh as a term unique to the early 21st century. But one thing can be said with confidence: healthy languages are endlessly fertile. They are capable of generating a constant stream of new words.

When the speakers of a language stop inventing new words, that language is in serious trouble. Many languages die out over time, and the lack of new words is often a sign of poor health. Right now, more languages are disappearing than at any previous moment in history. Indeed, the majority of the 6,000 or so languages spoken around the world may well have disappeared by the year 2100. The list of endangered languages is sadly long.

To: Dad & Mom
From: Alex Boswell
Sent: July 11
Subject: Wet day at camp

. . . .

Dear Mom and Dad,

It was pouring rain today, so instead of going out fossil hunting, we stayed inside and played games and sang camp songs. I kept pretty quiet. But a few people here are good singers. Noah's one of them—he grabbed hold of a guitar and played "**Kumbaya**." Afterward, he told us that the name of the song means "Come by here" in a special language that African-American people speak along the coast of South Carolina. I think he called it Gullah. He said that outsiders have often looked down on Gullah because it sounds so different from mainstream English. It's kind of lame that people could mock you just because of the way you speak…but then again it happened in my school last year, with a boy who'd just arrived from the Caribbean.

Keshia was nodding her head. She stood up and said her parents had brought her up to be proud of being black, and they'd passed on to her some English words that have African sources—not just slang but mainstream expressions, too. She gave **yam** as one example, **jazz** as another, and **coffee** as a third. But then Amina got upset because her uncle had told her that coffee was a proud Arabic word, and she started arguing with Keshia. Dr. Murray stood up finally and glared at us. When he glares, campers take notice.

After we'd all stopped talking, Dr. Murray told us that the origin of many words is lost in doubt. Coffee is one of them: it might come from Ethiopia, in eastern Africa, or it might come from Arabia. (And even if we found the fossil, it wouldn't necessarily tell us where the word was first used.) But wherever it started out, the word belongs to all of us now—just because you invent a word doesn't mean you control it. Origin is different from ownership. All languages are good, Dr. M added. We can be very proud of English, but that doesn't mean it's superior to other languages.

According to Dr. M, English now contains words and expressions from a huge number of other languages—more than 350, if you can believe it. (I didn't know there were that many languages in the world, but Noah tells me there are nearly twenty times that number. Wow!) Some people think this makes English a mongrel language, not a pure one, and Dr. M said he agreed. Except that being a mongrel is a compliment! Mongrel dogs are smart and adaptable—they usually live longer than purebreds and don't suffer from so many health problems. So when people say they want a language to be pure, they're not doing it any favors.

"But isn't it good to have a pure accent?" Steven asked. "You know, as opposed to a foreign one."

Dr. M's beard kept twitching like something was going on with his chin. "We all have an accent," he said. "And in some of the other countries where English is spoken, Steven, people might think your accent is downright peculiar."

Steven looked kind of shocked at that. But Dr. M paid no attention and just made the point again: nobody should claim that their type of English is better than anyone else's. The way the queens and kings of Britain talk was seen as ideal for centuries, but nowadays a lot of us think they sound weird, like something's blocking up their royal nostrils.

Then it was time for pasta and ice cream. After lunch, Dr. M told us more stuff about the history of the English language, but my fingers are getting tired so I won't repeat it now. I wish it would stop raining—Noah wants to lead us on a hike up Old English Hill.

Hope the move is going well. Don't waste time worrying about Jill and me!

Luv ya,

Alex

To: parents
From: Jillian Boswell
Sent: July 12
Subject: Little brother

· ·

Dear Mother and Father,

Since the last few days have failed to bring any sign that you're
planning to liberate me from this minimum-security prison, I assume
I will be stuck here for a few more weeks. It would be truly gratifying
to be free to do what I'd like to do, not what the counselors insist
I do. But you probably think that frustration is good for character-
building. Hah! In any case, I decided to write and tell you about a
recent event of some interest:
your son had an accident on
Old English Hill.

Don't be alarmed—he's not
seriously injured.

Alex is so gung-ho about
Camp Fossilized that he
was the first one outside
the cabins this morning.
I swear he would have
dashed up a mountain
at 6:00 a.m. if Noah
had asked him to. I
was a little late getting

going—I mean, really, how inconsiderate of me to want to sleep in until 8:00 a.m. on my summer vacation!—*not!*—and he came and banged on our windows. When you write to the wounded darling, you might want to inform him that the way to achieve popularity with a few reasonably cool teenage girls is not to shout threats at them in the early morning while nearly shattering their windows with your fists. Though if his main ambition in life is to rise to the dizzy heights of assistant camp counselor here in the sticks, he's following the right path.

Anyway. I staggered out to the kitchen for a few mouthfuls of that ridiculous meal called breakfast, and I was in more or less the same group as Alex when we started to climb a tall and ugly hill. I say "more or less" because I needed to talk to one or two interesting people at the back of the group, whereas Alex decided to out-Noah Noah and lead the charge up to the top, scratching his ears and turning over muddy stones and upending rocks as though his life depended on it. It must have been one of those rocks—I wasn't watching over him, you understand—that toppled sideways. Or maybe Alex was the one who toppled sideways. Anyway, he let out a very loud moan and began to sob—I mean, really.

Okay, I admit it, I'm being totally unfair, and he must have been in serious pain. I apologize. Noah and Kelly and a couple of other counselors bandaged up his ankle, conjured ice from a backpack, and generally made him feel less miserable. They informed me, as his next of kin, that his ankle is almost certainly not broken, and it's merely a Grade 2 sprain. After a while, with help, he was able to hobble down the hill. I stayed up on the peak with my friends for a

few more hours and, incidentally, I discovered the fossil for **weird**.
It comes from Old English, which means it's been hanging around in
the language for more than 1,000 years.

When we got back to camp, it was supper time and Alex was not
sobbing any longer. Thank goodness.

Your captive daughter,

Jill

To: Dad & Mom
From: Alex Boswell
Sent: July 12
Subject: left ankle

· ·

Dear Mom and Dad,

The worst thing happened today.

I was really happy this morning because when I woke up, the rain had stopped and the sunrise was fantastic: gold and purple streaks

of light over these wild high rocks. I love the badlands! Anyway, I tried to get everyone ready to leave on the big hike, but most people were still pretty sleepy. Especially in Jill's cabin. She made fun of me in front of my friends, again.

Before we set off, Noah told me that Old English Hill is just like the Old English language. At first, I didn't understand what he meant. It's an incredible formation—you can see it from our dining hall, and it looks like something out of a fantasy novel, with overhangs and huge boulders. But when you get up close, you find some clear paths to the top. Noah said the language is like that, too—it had a really flexible word order and a complicated grammar with lots of weird verbs, yet there was also a simplicity to it that made for some great poetry.

I just wanted to start fossil hunting! The other day, Dr. Murray said that compared to Indigenous Ridge, Old English Hill has way more fossils buried in unexpected places. This is where a lot of our basic words come from, right? So I climbed up all the way—the view from the summit is awesome—and even before most of the other guys had joined me, I'd already discovered a fossil. It was pretty heavy, and when I turned to ask Noah about it, it slipped out of my hands. I jerked my leg sideways and must have turned too hard on my left ankle. It hurt real bad, even worse than the time I fell down the stairs at school.

So now Noah tells me I have a sprained

ankle and won't be able to do any climbing for at least a week. Dr. Murray even asked if I wanted to go home. "No way!" I told him. (I didn't say that I don't really have a home at the moment.) The pain isn't too bad now, because they gave me some painkillers. What really hurts is the idea that the other campers will be climbing up French Mountain while I have to stay behind and rest my ankle.

Don't worry, I'll be fine. No, I don't want to leave camp! No way. I'll be climbing hills again soon, I swear.

By the way, you might want to ask Jill about this guy named Andreas…

gtg

Alex

p.s. Dr. Murray just told me that **ankle** comes from Old English but may have been affected by Old Norse, and some people think it's related to **claw** and other people think it's related to **knee**—but I don't want to think about all this right now. So he went away.

To: Michael Boswell, Karen Boswell
From: Steiner, Noah
Sent: July 12
Subject: Alex's sprain

. . . .

Dear Mr. and Mrs. Boswell,

I'm the counselor at Camp Fossil Eyes for your son, Alex. He's been having a wonderful time here, and with his enthusiasm for both nature and words, he has been contributing a lot to the camp's success.

Unfortunately, I have to tell you that today he sprained his left ankle and won't be able to participate in any of the field trips that are planned for the next several days. This is a shame, but I'm sure he will still enjoy himself. He'll be able to spend more time than usual with our camp director, Dr. Murray.

Alex suffered his injury this morning near the top of Old English Hill. I had explained to him that the fossils we'd find there belonged to the very earliest period of the English language. The term **English** is a good example because it refers to the Angles, a tribe who crossed the sea to Britain from their original homeland in Europe. They and another tribe, the

Saxons, were emigrants from what is now Germany, and the Old English language also goes by the name Anglo-Saxon. But I digress.

The campers learned today that Old English was spoken between about 700 and 1100. In its grammar, its vocabulary, even its alphabet, the language was very different from ours. I recited to Alex a few lines from *Beowulf*, the great epic poem of Old English: *Swa mec ge lome / laðgeteonan / þreatedon þearle.* This is an extinct language and, beyond doubt, a foreign one to people now. Even that short quotation is enough to show you that it had a few letters in its alphabet we don't use any longer. *Beowulf* was made into an action movie in 2007, so you may be familiar with the story. I digress again.

Alex was amazed to learn that this foreign language, this language that looks so peculiar to our eyes, is the source of hundreds of our most common and essential words (including **word** itself). Old English is, if you like, the bedrock of everything we say, even in the 21st century. Alex was exploring all this when he slipped and fell.

I'm sure you recall the form you both signed in May, excusing Camp Fossil Eyes from legal responsibility for any such events. However, I want to emphasize that we'll keep a close watch on your son during the next week and give him the best care we can.

Yours sincerely,

Noah Steiner

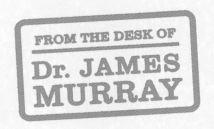
Three words from Old English

weird

Life could be short and cruel for the
Angles and Saxons. Warfare and
disease were common; antibiotics
did not exist. To maintain their
hope and peace of mind, knowing
they could die at any moment,
many people placed a huge weight
on the idea of destiny. Perhaps
it was their fate to accomplish
great things in life; perhaps it
was their fate to die young and
obscure. Their word for fate or destiny was *wyrd*.
The three *wyrdes* were the three Fates, supernatural
beings who were believed to shape the course of a life.

In the Early Middle Ages, between about 1100 and 1300,
Old English gradually evolved into what we call Middle
English. Hundreds of words died out over time, but
many hundreds of others survived, often with changes
in both their meaning and their spelling. That's a normal

process—few words have stayed exactly the same through the centuries. In Middle English, *wyrd* became **weird**, and it meant the ability to control a person's fate. If you were weird, you had supernatural abilities. That's what William Shakespeare meant when he used the word in his play *Macbeth* (written around 1605, when Middle English had evolved into Early Modern English). Shakespeare called a trio of witches "weird sisters." He wasn't commenting on how they looked; he was paying tribute to their power.

Another writer, Percy Shelley, seized hold of the word in 1815 and changed its meaning again. "In lone and silent hours," he wrote in the poem "Alastor," "when night makes a weird sound of its own stillness..." Gradually, the word would lose its supernatural associations and begin to mean simply "odd, peculiar, strange." That's how most people understand it today. Fate has nothing to do with it.

But language refuses to stay still. Many young people now use weird to describe someone who is interesting, out of the ordinary, or unconventional in a good way—a person who dresses, behaves, or talks in a way that doesn't fit the boring norm. From being a mild insult, weird may now be turning into a compliment. After all, few of us want to be exactly like everyone else in the crowd— although it's equally true that nobody likes to be identified as a **weirdo**. That word, which sprang to life in the 1950s, still counts as an attack.

gossip

The word **gossip** has been around for more than 1,000 years, but it has had several different meanings over the centuries. It began as the Old English combination of *God* and *sib*—in other words, a relative (our modern word **sibling**, meaning a brother or sister, also comes from *sib*). A "God relative" was a godfather or godmother: not a relative by blood, but an adult who solemnly promised to support and help the child being baptized.

A godparent would usually be a close and trusted friend of the family. And in the Middle English of the 14th century, gossip came to mean any good friend. Soon the word began to refer more and more to women friends, especially those women who were invited into a home to be present when a mother gave birth. (Throughout most of history, babies were born at home, not in hospitals.) The long hours of waiting gave busy women an excellent opportunity to talk to each other.

By 1600, the modern meaning of gossip was starting to emerge. It referred to a person, usually a woman, who liked to engage in conversation and who would pass along rumors and local news. A little later, it became a verb that meant to talk about other people's business; we still use it in that sense. But not until the 19th century did the noun make a further leap to mean the information (true or false) contained in those rumors—in other words, gossip stopped being the person telling the stories and became the stories being told.

A word with a somewhat similar meaning, **chatter**, entered the language in the 13th century (the Early Middle English period, experts call it). It took a few hundred years

before chatter was shortened to **chat**. Only recently, at the dawn of the 21st century, did the word **chatroom**—meaning an Internet site where people like to chat, chatter, and gossip—spring to life.

ladybug

Who would have thought a spotted insect owes its name to the Virgin Mary?

Hundreds of years ago, devout Christians named some of their favorite foodstuffs, plants, and animals after the mother of Jesus, whom they called "Our Lady." **Ladybugs** (or "ladybirds," as they're known in Britain) are among them. Similar names can be found not only in Britain but in other countries, too—in the German language, for instance, ladybugs are *Marienkäfer*, or "Mary beetles."

In Old English, before it was applied to the Virgin Mary, **lady** meant a bread maker. A *hlaefdige* (the origin of "lady") was literally a loaf-maid. The word *hlaef*, or "bread," eventually changed into "loaf," and *dige* (or *daege*) was a female servant or maid. Put those two short words together and you have a compound term that means a girl or woman who kneads bread. Gradually, *hlaefdige* came to mean the woman in charge of a household.

Time passed, pronunciations altered, and a *hlaefdige* became a *lafdi* or *lavede*: any woman with a high position in society. The word was like a badge of honor—only a small number of women would be recognized as ladies, just as a small number of men would qualify as "gentlemen." Even now, in the unlikely event that you

run across an
earl's daughter,
a knight's
widow, or the
wife of a duke's
younger son, you
should address
her as "Lady."

As for **bug**, it's a short word with a long and intricate
history (if you look it up in many dictionaries, you'll find
"origin unknown").

In modern English, it can refer to an insect, a system
fault, a snooping device, an illness, an enthusiasm—and
those are just the nouns. The most likely source is the Old
English word *budda,* meaning "beetle." Think of that the
next time your parents say, "Hey, bud!"

To: parents
From: Jillian Boswell
Sent: July 16
Subject: Obeying a request

· ·

Dear Mother and Father,

I have been given 15 minutes at the computer and told to write a message home. Which I am now doing. I'm such a dutiful daughter, yes?

Alexander is fine. You shouldn't be concerned. He is spending many hours with the Old Man of the Badlands, also known as Dr. Murray. If I know Alex like I think I do, he will soon be sending you an absurdly long message about the facts he has plucked from the leaky brain of that doddering, I mean distinguished, camp director. Alex might even feel that his injury is some kind of blessing in disguise because now he probably knows more about the history of words than any normal 13-year-old boy could imagine.

As for me, I am just back from climbing French Mountain, I need to take a shower, and I don't feel it is my role in the world to tell you everything that happens here. This is my life, not yours. But yes, I am learning things and no, I am not asking you to take me away. Not that you would even consider granting my request, based on the previous evidence.

My shower is calling. I can feel it.

Jill

p.s. I gather from your message to me that my gossiping brother has mentioned the name Andreas. He is a friend. I have other friends. Perhaps Alexander does not have enough friends?

To: Karen and Michael Boswell
From: Kelly Monahan
Sent: July 16
Subject: French Mountain

. . . .

Dear Mr. and Mrs. Boswell,

This is Kelly Monahan again, Jill's counselor. I'm writing in some frustration, I admit, because Dr. Murray asked the campers to send an e-mail home, telling their families about some of the things they've learned in the last few days. Most of the girls in my cabin did exactly that, but Jill admitted she failed to do so. To keep you as informed as all the other parents, I will now write a few quick paragraphs about French Mountain.

The campers and counselors left soon after sunrise this morning, and we drove in a few vans to the base of the mountain. It's pretty tall and is located some distance from camp. As soon as we arrived, several counselors, including myself, took turns telling the campers about the tremendous importance of French to the English language. Most of them were surprised to discover that at least a quarter of our language (including the words **surprised**, **discover**, **quarter**, and **language**) comes to us from French.

The reason is that England was conquered by an army from Normandy, in northern France, in 1066. The power, most of the wealth, and much of the land now lay in French hands. So even though Old English continued to be spoken for many years, especially by the peasants, it became essential for lots of people to learn French as well. Soon many French words began to flourish in English. One example is **nice**, which meant "ignorant" or "foolish" in Old French. Since coming into our language, it has gone through an incredible range of meanings: silly, cowardly, fussy, delicate, tasty, delightful, friendly… But when I spilled coffee on my jeans tonight and Jill said, "Nice!" I think she meant something else again.

As Jill and her friends began to climb the mountain, I showed them a way to grasp the enormous influence of French in those few critical centuries after 1066, when Old English was gradually giving way to Middle English. The word **cow** was used in Old English—yet **beef** arrived from French in the 13th century. **Pig** is also Old English—but **pork** moved in from French. **Sheep** goes back to Old English— whereas **mutton**, the meat of a sheep, comes from French. For a few hundred years, French speakers were the only people in Britain wealthy enough to be meat eaters, so it makes sense that their language supplied all these words for meat. Apart from various other items of **cuisine** (another French word), they introduced countless terms in fields like religion, government, and law.

Jill found three or four fossils on French Mountain. But what puzzled her and the others on the climb was that the writing on many of these fossils seemed incomplete. That's because a lot of French words actually began life in Latin, the language that was spoken all

across the Roman Empire 2,000 years ago. Latin is the source of all the Romance languages (French, Spanish, Italian, Portuguese, and several others) and by absorbing so many expressions from French and Latin, English fundamentally changed in character. Old English was purely a Germanic language, whereas Middle and Modern English are a hybrid—or a mongrel, as Dr. Murray likes to say.

I pointed to a nearby mountain that's even higher—we hope to climb it early next week—and I explained that its rocks are full of Latin fossils. So although the kids have learned a lot already, they may not know as much as they think. When it comes to word origins, the further back you go, the harder it is to decipher what the fossils are telling us and to be absolutely sure about their story.

Jill is in very good spirits, despite her refusal to write.

Best wishes,

Kelly

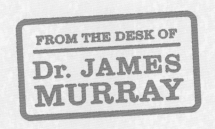

Three words from French

umpire

Over the course of
history, some words
have had plenty of
meanings but a single
spelling. Other words
have kept their meaning
intact despite major changes in how they're spelled and
pronounced. One of them is **umpire**. It began its career in
this language more than 650 years ago, arising from the
Old French word *nonper*.

A *nonper* was someone who judged a dispute. He or she
was not (*non*) an equal (*per*) of either side. In its first
recorded appearance in Middle English, the word was
spelled *noumpere*. The central meaning has stayed the
same since then: a person who is given the power to
decide between two competing forces. Nowadays, we're
likely to think of an umpire as a referee in a game of
baseball, tennis, or cricket. But the word can also be used
in business and law.

How did we get from a *noumpere* to an umpire? The answer involves a process that linguists call "false splitting." It's easy for us to forget that most speakers of English throughout history couldn't read or write. When they heard talk of a *noumpere*, they didn't know what letter the main word was supposed to begin with. Often they assumed it should begin with an *o* or a *u*, not with the letter *n*. Similar cases of false splitting turned a French *naperon* into an English **apron** and an Arabic *nāranj* into a French and English **orange**.

False splitting can work the other way, too. In the Middle Ages, a village in England might have contained a dozen men named John. They were told apart from each other not by their family names but by an *eke* name, *eke* being an old word for extra: John the Wise, John the Tall, John the Lazy, and so on. Not realizing they should be talking about an *eke* name, people began to hear the phrase as "a *neke* name"—which explains why, hundreds of years later, we say a **nickname**.

sabotage

French continued to provide the English language with a stream of new words even into the 20th century. **Sabotage**, for

instance, arrived in 1910. It means to undermine, disrupt, or destroy the normal operations of a company or country, especially by violent or illegal methods. The people who do the disrupting are called **saboteurs**, a term that is often applied to workers involved in a bitter labor dispute or to guerrillas in time of war.

But at the root of the word is, of all things, a wooden shoe.

Sabot has been the name of a French wooden shoe ever since the 13th century. And if you've ever tried walking about in wooden shoes, you'll know they make a loud and ugly sound. The French verb *saboter* first meant to walk noisily, and then, by extension, it came to mean to bungle something or mess it up—if you were playing a piano sonata, for instance, and you banged your elbow on the keys. From there, it was a small leap to the notion of sabotage: messing something up on purpose.

Sometimes people like to invent colorful histories for words, as if the true stories aren't good enough. It has been suggested that sabotage derives from a real-life incident in which striking workers took off their wooden shoes and hurled them into a factory's machines. Yet there's no evidence that anything like this ever occurred. You can find the story on the Internet, but it's unlikely to be true.

bikini

On July 1, 1946, the United
States tested an atomic bomb
at Bikini Atoll, part of the
Marshall Islands chain in the
South Pacific. The explosion
was the first of many over the
next 12 years. Before the test,
the islanders who lived on Bikini
were removed from their homes—
supposedly on a temporary basis,
although even now the island
remains uninhabited. Coming less than a year after the
end of World War Two, the explosion made headlines
around the world.

On July 5, 1946, two men named Louis Réard and
Jacques Heim introduced a new kind of swimsuit at a
fashion show in Paris. Earlier that year, a one-piece suit
called an Atome (from the French word for "atom") had
been advertised as "the smallest bathing suit in the world."
If the American explosion had occurred a week later, it's
unclear what name Réard and Heim would have given
to their creation. But as the atom had just been split on
Bikini, and as their new two-piece suit covered even less
than an Atome, the Frenchmen decided to call the suit
a **bikini**.

The word took off, not just in French but in countless languages, including English. Other terms would later be formed using bikini as a basis—**tankini**, for example, for a two-piece swimsuit with a tank top.

There's more to the word's success than luck and brilliant marketing. The name Bikini comes from the South Pacific language of Marshallese (it's said to combine the Marshallese terms for "surface" and "coconut"). But in most European languages, *bi* is associated with the number two. A bicycle has two wheels; a bilingual person speaks two languages; bifocal glasses improve both near and far vision. What better choice for a two-piece swimsuit than a noun beginning with *bi*?

To: Dad & Mom
From: Alex Boswell
Sent: July 18
Subject: badlands & other stuff

· ·

Dear Mom and Dad,

I guess you've finished the move by now, and I hope it's gone really well. Sorry not to have written you a letter in the last few days. Thx for your messages. I've been busy!

You probably want to know about my ankle. I've been doing a lot of exercises— stretching my leg, lifting my foot, that kind of thing—and it's getting stronger all the time. I had to miss the Nordic field trip today, which I'm sad about, and I may not be able to go on the big Latin hike. But Noah says I should be fine for the last couple of trips.

So what have I been up to? Well, I've had time to hang out with Dr. Murray, who's told me all kinds of stuff about the English language.

Did you know that **abominable snowman** is a bad translation from Tibetan? (*Mi t'om* means man-bear, *k'ang mi* means snowfield man, but the translators got mixed up.) Anyway, the first thing Dr. Murray did, the day after my injury, was to have me hobble outside the main building into a small garden where they grow corn, beans, and a few other plants. I wondered if he wanted me to do some weeding, but instead he raised his eyebrows and said, "Find a fossil!"

I poked around and looked here and there. In fact, I nearly uprooted a few plants before Dr. M said, "Try your luck near the far wall." And there it was—the fossil of **badlands**, in two connected segments just like the word itself. I thought the history would be fairly obvious, but Dr. M shook his head and told me otherwise. The most innocent-

looking words sometimes come with unpredictable stories, and **bad** is one of them. It started off meaning "inferior" or "defective," but these days some people use it when they want to say something is totally excellent. **Land** has meant the soil or the ground for more than 1,000 years—that's the gist of what Dr. Murray said. I didn't really understand the way he related the word to Middle Welsh, Old Irish, Frisian, and a bunch of other languages but, believe me, he did.

Put "bad" and "lands" together, and you get the word that describes these amazing formations—the erosion has produced strange rock shapes and patterns. Simple, right? Except that before I put the fossil back where I'd found it, Dr. Murray asked me to turn it over. And on the other side, I could see something different—the writing made it look like French was involved. Dr. M explained that although badlands is an American term dating from the 19th century, it was also a direct translation of the French expression *mauvaises terres*. And the French might have borrowed the idea from an indigenous language in North America. So what seems like a straightforward English word ends up being pretty complicated.

After we went inside, Dr. Murray talked to me about his whole philosophy of language. He thinks the reason so many people want words to stay still, and to have a single meaning that never varies, is that they're scared of language change. They like the idea of a Dictionary—"with a capital *D*," he said—that will tell them exactly what a word means and how it should be used. But that's not how English works. A spelling can be right in one country and wrong in another. Pronunciations can be crazy different—when Dr. M puts on a Scots accent, I can barely understand a word he says. And as

I've been learning for the past couple of
weeks, meanings are always ready
to morph. I mean change.

But if we know what to look
for, we can discover an
awful lot, not just
about old words but
also about the
people who used
them. That's one
of the reasons
that Dr. M decided
to call the camp
"Fossil Eyes." When
we contemplate language, he said,
we see the past in a very sharp and focused way.
We don't just look *at* a word; we look *through* the word into the
past. Go back far enough, and you find that **salary** was the money a
soldier was given to buy salt. It was the main way of making sure
food didn't rot. That gives us an idea of how valuable salt used to be!

Well, I gotta go—did you understand that last word in my e-mail a
few days ago?

cu

Alex

To: parents
From: Jillian Boswell
Sent: July 18
Subject: Old Norse

. . . .

Hello parents,

Kelly has been giving me serious grief for not describing to you all
the things I'm doing, I mean learning, and I am tired of her continual
small lectures and big, sad eyes. So, under protest, I will now inform
you about some things that happened earlier today. I know that
Alex missed out on climbing Nordic Spur, and therefore you won't
be hearing anything about its fossils from his large mouth. So I
will tell you the following (but don't blame me if it's not perfectly
organized—I'm a 15-year-old girl, not a supergeek):

* The French conquered England and settled down there in 1066.
The Vikings didn't do that—they just sailed out of their homeland
in Scandinavia, raiding and pillaging and other fun stuff, and then

sailed off to attack somebody
else. That's why English doesn't
have as many words from the
Viking language, Old Norse, as it
does from French.

* Except that some of those
words are really key ones, like
they and **their**. So, contrary to
what I just wrote, the Vikings didn't

just raid and pillage: some of them settled down, especially in the north of England. And when they did, they hauled some language along with them.

* Like **anger**. Keshia, who is the most amazing person at finding fossils—I honestly don't know how she does it—was talking to me near the bottom of Nordic Spur (*spur* is an Old Norse word, by the way) when her eyes suddenly went blank. She gave a little shout, took three steps, and pulled this rock out of the ground. It turns out that when the Vikings said *angr*, they meant "grief" or "sorrow." Lots of other people were angry at the Vikings and sorry when they showed up.

* **Ugly** also comes from Old Norse, and the boy who noticed its fossil today certainly fits that description, but being a sweet-natured person I won't mention his name. When the Vikings were around, they used *uggligr*—isn't that an ugly-looking word?—to describe something that was truly frightening and utterly horrible.

* I found three fossils on Nordic Spur, even though the afternoon was brutally hot, so I am quite pleased with myself. One of them was a beautiful oval-shaped rock, and at first I didn't even realize it was a fossil. Then I understood: I was holding **egg**. Long ago, the word was *ei*, but I guess it finally found a consonant it could live with. I turned it over and over in my hand.

Okay, I believe that is more than enough for a single letter. I saw Alex limping around camp an hour ago and I waved at him. He waved back, sort of.

Goodbye parents,

Jill

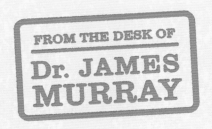

Two words from Old Norse

berserk

The extinct language of
Old Norse was spoken
by the Vikings and
their descendants
between about 800
and 1300. Several
modern languages
emerged from it:
Norwegian, Icelandic,
Faroese, Swedish, and
Danish. (Icelandic has remained closest
to its Viking ancestor.) Linguists put all these tongues
together in a larger group they call North Germanic—
which means that the Scandinavian languages, including
Old Norse, are distant cousins of German, Dutch, and
English. The Romance languages, including French and
Latin, form a separate family.

The Viking word berserk is an interesting example of
a word that disappeared for centuries before being

rediscovered. In Old Norse, the word *berserkr* came from *bera serka*, or "bear shirt." Clothed in a bear's skin, a Viking *berserkr* would rush into fearless combat. He would be caught up in the frenzy of battle, and sometimes he would even survive. But after a few hundred years of raiding, the Vikings settled down and became peaceable farmers and sailors. And the term *berserkr* was forgotten. But then the Scottish writer Sir Walter Scott described "Berserkars" in his 1822 novel *The Pirate*. Scott's writing was so popular that the word was reborn.

Today, we occasionally hear about a person "going berserk." That phrase dates back to 1867, a few decades after the publication of Scott's book. To go berserk is to lose your emotional balance and enter a destructive frenzy—although occasionally people use the phrase in a lighter context, such as "She went berserk at the sight of Johnny Depp." The meaning is very similar to that of other phrases like "run amok" and, more recently, "go postal."

sky

When you come across a one-syllable word beginning with *sc-* or *sk-*, odds are it started off in Old Norse. **Skill**, **skin**, **scare**, and **score** are a few examples. Another Old Norse word that made its way into English was *ský*. But a Norse *ský* was never blue or starry—because the meaning of *ský* was "cloud."

Old English had a word of its own for the **sky**, *welkin*. Geoffrey Chaucer, Britain's leading poet in the 1300s, once wrote that a strong wind "left not a sky / In all the welkin"—or, to put it into modern English, the wind "didn't leave a cloud in the sky." In Old Norse, *ský* is related to *skugge*, the word for "shadow." By 1600, the original meaning of sky had vanished.

Today, the old word "welkin" has pretty much vanished, too. But welkin, just like sky, was related to words in other languages that mean clouds, damp, and moisture. Maybe England's soggy climate was the reason that people began to use welkin and then sky to mean everything in the upper air, not just the gray and rainy parts. A more likely reason is that people used to think Earth lay directly under Heaven, where the weather would never be wet and miserable. If you looked up, you could glimpse the home of God—as long as it wasn't blanketed by clouds.

In modern times, several sky-related phrases have appeared. A **sky marshal** (an armed guard on airplanes) dates from the 1960s. A decade later, some people began to call police helicopters **sky bears**. When it comes to inventing fresh expressions, the sky's the limit. That is to say: there *is* no limit.

To: Dad & Mom
From: Alex Boswell
Sent: July 20
Subject: unique word

. . . .

Dear Mom and Dad,

How are you? Still unpacking, I guess. I want you to know that I'm doing fine. In fact, I'm doing better than fine. I found something really amazing on a short hike today. Noah, who was with me, said he'd never seen anything like it.

We were walking through a low stretch of the badlands about 10 minutes away from camp—Noah wanted me to test my ankle before I try climbing again. And I suddenly noticed a strange-looking stone glittering in the sun. We went over and pulled it out. But Noah had no idea where it came from. He looked at the faint writing and insisted it wasn't an Indo-European word, whatever that means. He turned and looked over his shoulder, even though there was nobody around, and then he carefully lifted the fossil into his backpack and carried it to camp.

He was a little nervous that Dr. Murray would be mad at him for bringing a fossil back with him, but Dr. M didn't mind at all (as long as Noah returned it to exactly the same place). He stroked his beard a few times and then it was as though a light went on in his eyes. "Ah yes," he said. "A word from Nenets. The word from Nenets. The *only* word from Nenets!"

The fossil was **parka**—weird, discovering it on such a hot day. Turns out that the word has a strange history. No wonder Noah couldn't decipher it! The Nenets are a reindeer-herding people in north-western Siberia, where it can get unbelievably cold in winter and you

need a hooded deerskin coat to survive. The Nenets language belongs to the Uralic family, which has absolutely no connection with ours—the grammar, as well as the vocabulary, is totally different. But a few hundred years ago, the Nenets passed their word for hooded coat on to the Russians they met, and when Russian sailors made it to the Aleutian Islands, between Asia and North America, they transferred the term to the indigenous people there. In turn, the Aleuts mentioned their *parki* (made of bird skins, not reindeer) to visiting Americans—which is how the word got into English.

Dr. Murray said that, in his opinion, the story proves a key point about English. Plenty of other languages have an academy to govern them—there are actually people who decide whether or not a word should be allowed to enter that particular language. Or if a brand-new word is needed, like when the latest item of technology arrives on the market, these people are supposed to invent a word for it. France has one of these academies, so does Turkey and so does Israel. I said this had to be the coolest job in the world, but Dr. M shook his head. He said that ours has always been a free language, accepting words from anywhere and everywhere, regardless of their family of origin. If English had been controlled by some academy, a word from a reindeer-herders' language in Siberia might never have received permission to enter.

Oh no, I'm late for supper.

xoxo

Alex

To: Michael Boswell, Karen Boswell
From: Steiner, Noah
Sent: July 21
Subject: Dutch treat

· ·

Dear Mr. and Mrs. Boswell,

This is Noah Steiner again. I'm sending this message at Alex's request. He says he wrote to you yesterday, and this evening he's pretty tired. But he wanted you to know the good news: he successfully climbed a steep hill today, and I'm confident he'll be able to join our long hike into the Greek Mountains on the weekend.

This morning he and I, along with another boy named Steven, waited until the other campers had left for the Latin Alps before we walked over to Dutch Hill. On the way, Alex asked me a very good question: Why should we search for Dutch or Greek fossils when there are other languages in the world that are spoken by far more people?

The answer is that most of those "big" languages—Chinese, Arabic, Hindi, and Russian, for example—didn't contribute as much to the growth of English. Sure, we've scooped up words from all of them, but we haven't scooped nearly as many as we have from a small language like Dutch. That said, there are certainly some expressions from those other languages that made their way into English. Campers who are staying here for the month of August will get a chance to search them out. I'm particularly keen on **algebra**, **algorithms**, **alchemy**, and other scientific words that come from Arabic. But I digress.

I told the boys that hundreds of years ago the Netherlands was rich, powerful, and just a short sea journey away from the coast of England. The Dutch were a great seafaring people. So they were in close contact with the British—and with Americans, too. Don't forget: New York was once New Amsterdam! The Dutch depended on trade, and they traded words and ideas as well as objects. Overall, their language ranks fifth among all foreign tongues when we measure the number of words they have given English. Only French, Latin, Greek, and Old Norse have provided us with more.

As we started to climb the hill, I told the boys to look out for Dutch words related to the sea. **Yacht**, **buoy**, and **dock** are a few examples. But as luck would have it, the boys found other kinds of fossils. Steven was the first to spot one, lurking at the entrance to a cave:

booze, which lots of kids think is modern slang. It isn't—the word has been around for more than 700 years. Before it arrived in English, *busen* (to drink heavily) was already a verb in Dutch. "You keep telling us about all these words that change their meaning," Alex said to me. "But some words stay the same!" He was right.

A few minutes later, he and Steven let out a shout at almost the same moment. I had to laugh when I saw the fossils they'd unearthed. Alex had got hold of **pickle**, while Steven had found **cookie**. Before a cookie became a treat in North American kitchens—and long before it was a computer term for data sent to and from a server—it was a *koekje*, meaning "little cake" in Dutch. As for pickle, it goes all the way back to 1400, and the first English meaning of it was a spicy gravy for meat. The Dutch word *pekel* referred to a brine for preserving food—in those days there were no refrigerators or freezers, so it was hard to keep food from spoiling. Eventually, a pickle came to mean a cucumber or other vegetable soaked in brine.

But the word isn't merely about food. In British slang, if you're in a pickle, you're in some kind of trouble. The Dutch expression *in de pekel zitten* (in the pickle sit) also means being in trouble. So in all likelihood we borrowed the Dutch phrase, not just the individual word. This is an appalling digression, I'm sorry.

Alex and Steven found other fossils, too, but those were the ones they liked the most. They clambered down the hill, shouting, "In the pickle, sit!" over and over again. I had to remind myself that they *are* only 13.

I think we can be confident that Alex will enjoy his final week at Camp Fossil Eyes. Of course, he'll be delighted to see you again. Lately he's been missing you both.

Sincerely,

Noah Steiner

To: parents
From: Jillian Boswell
Sent: July 21
Subject: Salutations, parents

. . . .

Hey there—

Both the words in my subject line
come from Latin, if you didn't already
know. A bunch of big words come
from Latin. Well, I know **parents** isn't
an especially big word but it carries a
heavy weight. That's a joke, haha, I'm
not implying anything. Today we did a
lot of climbing in the Latin Alps and the
views were **stupendous**. Which is another Latin word. There are so
many. It wasn't just the main language of the Roman Empire but also
of European civilization—for a long, long time. So English sort of
bulked up on Latin terminology.

I believe Alex was going Dutch today—good for him. It's a pleasant
hill, I'm told. We had an awesome time in the mountains. I was hiking
with my friend Andreas and what did he find? **Universe**. I thought
that was so great: he could pick up a rock and hold the world in
the palm of his hand. In Latin, universe literally meant "turned into
one." That's what Kelly told us, anyway. All the random fragments of
existence, gathered together into a single whole. Her eyes went a
little misty.

Andreas goes to a high school where he can take Latin. Can you find me a school like that? He says there used to be thousands of schools that taught Latin because for centuries it was the essential language of culture and politics and education. In fact, you could say that because of the Roman Empire and the Roman Catholic Church, Latin was the first real stab at a global language. But now most schools have abandoned it. I think that's a shame.

Do you **remember**—Latin again! well, Latin and French—when I was in kindergarten and had my appendix taken out? This afternoon I turned over a cute fossil on a steep slope and Kelly told me it was **appendix**. She said it meant a little text attached to the end of a

book, before doctors started using the word in the 17th century to mean this useless little organ attached to the end of my stomach. I hope it was useless, anyway, because I'll never get it back.

Yes, well, you **probably** (Latin) want me to be terribly **serious** (Latin again) but hey, it's summertime, right? And the living should be easy.

Your **devoted** (joke?) (Latin!) daughter,

Jill

p.s. Dr. Murray just stopped by and asked me if I realized that the name "Jillian" is derived from Latin. He said it means "youthful." Which is cool. But will I have to change my name when I get old?

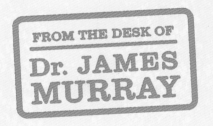

Three words from Latin

propaganda

A work of **propaganda** aims to
influence what people think by
telling part of the truth while
disguising or hiding the rest.
To see how it became a word in
English, we need to travel back into the past.

Nearly 2,000 years ago, at the peak of its power, the
Roman Empire stretched over a vast territory, including
most of western, southern, and central Europe, part
of North Africa, and some of western Asia. The rulers
of the empire did not always hail from Italy—emperors
were born in what are now Morocco, Spain, France, Libya,
Turkey, Greece, and Serbia. It was a multinational empire
that functioned in the Latin language, and it lasted for
centuries. But finally, battered by waves of invaders from
the north, it fell apart in the 5th century.

The main reason its language remained so important is
that before the empire collapsed, its leaders had adopted

Christianity as the official religion. That decision made Latin the language of the church. And through most of its history, all over the world, the Roman Catholic Church held its services in Latin.

In the centuries after the empire's fall, much of what the Romans knew and wrote was forgotten—that's why people spoke about the Dark Ages. Yet a knowledge of Latin endured. This knowledge would be essential to the Renaissance (a French word, literally meaning "rebirth"), which shaped the early modern world. Great scientists like Isaac Newton, who discovered gravity, chose to write in Latin. As late as the 18th century, Latin was a global battleground of ideas.

What does all this have to do with propaganda? Well, in 1622 Pope Gregory XV founded the *Sacra Congregatio de Propaganda Fide*—the holy congregation for the increasing of the faith. In Latin, propaganda meant "spreading" or "increasing." It didn't suggest anything bad until the early 20th century, when some political movements and governments began to use powerful methods of persuasion that distorted the truth. Needing a word for such practices, people remembered the church's propaganda.

interface

The Latin word *facies* (appearance, form, or figure) is the source of the English word **face**. The obvious meaning, from the 13th century onward, has been the front of a person's head. Dozens of common expressions rely on the word. Some of them are physical, such as "to pull a

face" (to make an unpleasant grimace). But the majority are metaphorical: "losing face" (suffering embarrassment or humiliation), "saving face" (avoiding embarrassment), "out of face" (in a bad mood), and so on. In a hockey game, a **face-off** occurs when two players on opposite teams come face-to-face for a dropping of the puck. "Face" can also be a verb that means to look at something without flinching. If you have to "face the music," you don't turn away from punishment.

The word can also be a synonym for surface, as in "the moon's hidden face." And when scientists in the 19th century needed a word for the surface that forms the common boundary between two materials, they chose **interface**—a compound word that draws on two Latin roots. The first, *inter*, is Latin for "between." It's found at the start of many words, such as **international** and **interracial**. **Internet** combines a Latin prefix with an Old English noun.

As a scientific term, interface was fairly rare. Not many people understood it. But in the 1960s, the author and philosopher Marshall McLuhan grabbed the word by the scruff of its neck and gave it a new meaning. He wrote about "the interface of the Renaissance," by which he meant the coming together of modern and medieval outlooks. Before long, a writer for *Scientific American* suggested that "the issue of insanity as a defense in criminal cases...is at the interface of medicine, law and ethics." But the term really took off in the realm of computers, where it now means the point of interaction between two systems, such as a printer and a hard drive.

Whereas words that come from Anglo-Saxon and Old Norse are usually short, Latin-based words are often long. Sometimes, bad writers use interface as a pompous replacement for simpler words like **meet**. Politicians who want to hide the truth make heavy use of Latin-based words. Milton Smith, an American who invented **bafflegab** to mean "pretentious language," gave a tongue-in-cheek definition: "multiloquence characterized by consummate interfusion of circumlocution or periphrasis, inscrutability, and other familiar manifestations of abstruse expatiation..." Most of Smith's long words come from Latin.

manure

"Manure your heart with diligence, and in it sow good seed," wrote Zachary Boyd, an obscure Scottish poet, in 1645. What in the world was he thinking about?

Like people, words occasionally take a spectacular tumble. The history of **manure** is a case in point: it's the verbal equivalent of an Olympic athlete aiming for an elegant dive and performing a belly flop instead. Its source is a Latin phrase, *manu operari*, meaning "to work with the hands"—we owe words like **manual** to *manus* (hand), and words like **operation** to *operari* (work). But like many English words with a Latin origin, this one first had to pass through French, changing into *manouvrer* and entering English around 1400.

From being a verb for general work that involved the hands, manure took on the particular sense of working the earth and cultivating the land—in other words, improving or developing it. It became a farmer's term. By the late 16th century, manure had come to mean putting dung on the soil to fertilize it. And from there, it turned into a noun: the dung that farmers mixed into the soil. For a time, that meaning coexisted with the earlier idea of training or developing something, including a heart or a mind. But the new meaning crowded out the old ones.

So Zachary Boyd wasn't telling his readers to mix dung into their hearts but to make them better. And that Latin phrase, *manu operari*, would be filtered through French and into English all over again. The second time round, it gave rise to an English word with a parallel history but a very different meaning: **maneuver**.

To: Dad & Mom
From: Alex Boswell
Sent: July 22
Subject: checkmate

. . . .

Just a quick note to tell you about this amazing fossil I saw today.
We had camp cleanup this morning—boring!—but luckily, Noah
took a few of us for a drive in the late afternoon. We went over to
Persian Hill—not much of a hill, to be honest, more like a large
bump. That's no reflection on the Persian language, which Noah said
is ancient and beautiful, nor on the modern-day country of Iran. It's
just that Persian hasn't given too many words to English.

I was hardly out of my seatbelt before I saw Keshia holding up this
gorgeous fossil: **checkmate**. If you take the word back through

Middle English, French, and Arabic, you get to the Persian phrase *shāh māt*—"the king died." Which sums up the end of a chess game, right? Noah said that until the late 20th century, the ruler of Iran was still known as the Shah. The fossil was beautiful—it seemed to glitter in the sun.

"Let's see if you can get hold of **paradise**, too," Noah said, with a grin. "It's got a fantastic history." Way back in time, he told us, it was *pairidaēza*—a Persian word that meant a wall around a garden or an orchard. Later it came to refer to the garden itself, especially the Garden of Eden. Today people are more likely to talk about paradise when they imagine an empty beach by a warm sea. But we only had a few minutes, and with the dust flying around in the wind, we couldn't find the fossil.

We *did* see—oh no, there are six people waiting to use the computer…

A.

Dear Mom and Dad,

Today we had another unplanned field trip—and I was one of the people who got to go on it. As my friend Steven would say: "Woot!"

It was supposed to be a rest day before our long hike into the Greek Mountains. But the weather was beautiful this morning, fairly cool, and Dr. Murray suddenly called us together and said he was feeling guilty. He said it wasn't fair that the campers who'd be leaving in a week would have missed the chance to explore one of the most exciting sources of new words in English—one that had given us some old words, too.

So, he said, he'd spoken to Noah, and Noah had agreed to take the first eight volunteers down to Spanish Mesa. You can bet my hand shot up. Steven and Keshia came, too, along with a few people I don't know so well, but Jill chose to stay behind. Speaking as her brother, I get the feeling she's not really into words right now.

First we headed down a narrow trail, and in the shadows the mosquitoes were really bad. Noah stopped to inform us that **mosquito** means "little fly" in Spanish. He was telling us something more complicated—about how mosquito and **musket** have the same Latin root, *musca*—when he got so badly bitten on his neck he gave up and moved on. Next up was a huge kind of hat, **ten gallon**, which he said was also a Spanish term.

"Huh?" I said. "It sounds totally English."

"Yeah, but try putting 10 gallons of water or anything else on your head," Noah replied. "You'd be wearing a trash can. Nobody's 100 percent sure about this, but probably one or two of the early cowboys in Texas heard the Spanish phrase *tan galan*—'how gallant!'—and translated it wrong. A lot of words develop from a mistake."

"Hey!" Keshia called over to him. "What's this?"

As usual, she was the first to notice a fossil. Noah looked worried at first and kept scratching his ear because he was having trouble working out its meanings, but then he cheered up and told her she'd found **ranch**. He said she might have come across it on French Mountain, too, because not all its history is Spanish. But starting with the French verb *ranger* (arrange or install), it moved into Spain—at first it meant to be lodged somewhere, then it meant a bunch of

people who eat together. Finally it crossed over to Mexico, where it ended up as *rancho,* a "little farm." Today, of course, ranches are for cattle or other large animals, and they can be enormous.

So we started to climb the mesa—a flat-topped hill, basically. I didn't realize how steep it would be, and I don't think Noah did either. After we'd been hiking for 10 or 15 minutes, Steven was so out of breath he couldn't take another step. Noah decided we should rest and then go down again, and nobody was too upset, not even Keshia. Besides, when we'd come most of the way down, she noticed this area just off to our right that was full of fossils. We'd been so busy climbing that we hadn't seen it on the way up.

The fossils were closely packed together. I found **enchilada**, Keshia got hold of **burrito** and **guacamole**, Steven grabbed **churro**…

all these food words in a small space, including a few I'd never heard of. (Sometime we should try eating **natillas**—you know my sweet tooth, right?) Noah explained that American English is now scarfing down a whole bunch of Spanish words, and not all of them are about food. Some Americans are even getting scared there's too much Spanish in their English. Noah said that a couple of years ago, a cable-news show asked Dr. M to go into a studio and talk about the danger of Spanish words invading our language. But Dr. M said it was no big deal because English has always lifted expressions from other places—and besides, a lot of people in Latin America are upset about all the English words showing up there.

I'm looking forward to the last week of camp. But it'll be great to see you both again. I miss you!

xoxoxoxoxo

Alex

To: parents
From: Jillian Boswell
Sent: July 24
Subject: Fantastic

. . . .

Dear parents,

This may be the last message I send before you drag me away from here (joke?) and I'm writing it at the end of a truly amazing day. Andreas was excited to find out about Greek words because two of his grandparents were born in Greece and he loves listening to them talk—he only wishes he could reply more fluently. The fossils we found today come from Ancient Greek, not Modern, but some Greek words haven't changed that much in the last 2,000 years.

We set off at sunrise because it took us a while to reach the Greek Mountains. They loom up behind the Latin Alps. Kelly said the Romans were in awe of the Greek civilization that had sprung up before their own, and they imported a lot of Greek ideas and words into their own language. Apparently, there's a whole region we didn't have time to explore today where the fossils contain chunks of both languages—like **television**, which is kind of a sandwich word, first bite Greek, second bite Latin.

At first Andreas and I stayed with Kelly, Amina, and one or two other people, but then we headed off on our own—not for long, dear parents, don't tie yourselves in a knot. If you think I'm being sarcastic, maybe you're right—I found the fossil for **sarcasm** below this silvery bush at the side of the trail. Andreas can read Greek, which uses a different alphabet than we do, and he remembered hearing that the Greek word *sarkazein* (to sneer or speak bitterly) literally means "to rip away flesh." *Sarkos* is flesh. Hmm.

We also found the fossil for **demon**. The Greeks gave us tons of cool words for things you really don't want to experience, both small scale (**parasites**) and huge scale (**catastrophes**). But for them, a demon was just a divine force or spirit—we're the ones who transformed it into an evil monster.

When we linked up again with Kelly and the crew, Amina found a fossil that nearly made us die laughing. It was **gorilla**. And no, I'm not joking. Kelly said most people assume that the word comes straight from an indigenous language, like **chimpanzee** and **orangutan** do. But the animal wasn't even named—I mean by English speakers; there would have been lots of names for it in

African languages!—until 1847. The guy who did the naming was a missionary named Reverend Savage. No joke again. He'd read an Ancient Greek translation of a book by an explorer who set out from Carthage, on the Mediterranean Sea, around 500 BC. When this explorer, whose name was Hanno the Navigator, sailed down the west coast of Africa, he ran into what he called *gorillai*.

Or maybe he just saw them from a distance. Because Hanno didn't realize they were animals—he thought they were wild and hairy women. Reverend Savage remembered the story and the Greek translation when he needed an English word for this new type of wild and hairy ape.

Oh well, it all goes to show that the better you know the old classics, the easier it is to come up with new words for what you find. If I ever bump into an undiscovered species, I plan to bear this in mind.

And on that note, I will stop. Greek really is a **fantastic** language, you know. (As in *phantastikos*—capable of imagining. Kelly didn't tell me that; Andreas did.)

You would be fantastic parents if you let me stay here for another month. Andreas's parents might let him stay. He's asking them.

Jill

To: Dad & Mom
From: Alex Boswell
Sent: July 24
Subject: My name is cool

· ·

Dear Mom and Dad,

I'm wiped, having climbed all day in the Greek Mountains— who would have thought a word camp would be such a good workout? This won't be a long message. Hope you don't mind. But I'll be seeing you soon anyway.

I wanted to tell you I found my name! I still don't know if Noah arranged it somehow, or if it was total coincidence. But high up on a ridge, where Daniel and I were eating our sandwiches while looking across the badlands, it suddenly felt like one of the rocks was calling out to me. I'd never had that feeling before, but Keshia told me it's how she finds so many fossils—she has some kind of sixth sense for the moment when she'll discover something. That's how it was for me today. The rock broke free from the gravel, and when I turned it over, I knew it was something special. Noah ran right up when I shouted to him, and he told me about **Alexander**.

It combines two parts. The second, from *andros*, means "man." The first is a little trickier—it's from *alexein*, which can mean "defend," or "protect," or "keep something bad away." Put the two together, and you get "protector of men" or "defender of men." I don't suppose Jill would be overly impressed, but I think it's a fantastic name to have… so thank you!

Noah told Daniel he should be proud of his name, too: it means "God is my judge" in the Hebrew language. Daniel said he would have preferred to be a defender of men, but at least his name doesn't mean skunk land or something.

One last field trip and then I'll be home—

ta4n,

Alex

p.s. In case you were wondering, "that's all for now."

p.p.s. Am I a smart aleck? Back in the 19th century, when that term was born, somebody with my name must have been.

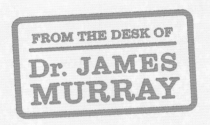

Three words from Greek

catastrophe

Writers and scholars in the
European Renaissance looked
to the Greek and Roman
cultures of the past as a
source of knowledge and a
fountain of wisdom. They
feared that their own
languages, such as English
and French, were shabby

compared to the great classical tongues
of long ago. When they wanted to express new concepts,
they scoured Greek and Latin texts for inspiration.

Catastrophe is one of the many words that arrived in
English during the Renaissance. In the 16th century,
theater was becoming a popular art form in Europe.
But people had no word to express a surprising change
of fortune near the climax of a play. Wanting to create
such a word, they looked back to the Ancient Greek verb
katastrephein (to overturn). A catastrophe didn't have to

be bad; it merely had to be unexpected. As the playwright John Gay wrote: "They deny it to be tragical, because its catastrophe is a wedding." He was not suggesting that the marriage was doomed.

The word was too useful to remain limited to the theater. By 1750, catastrophe was losing its positive side and had come to mean any sudden, surprising disaster. Then it became a synonym for disaster, whether or not the disaster was surprising. In the 1850s, geologists began to speak of **catastrophism** as a theory that might explain some puzzling episodes in Earth's history. A word born in the arts had come to express a scientific idea: that a few violent events of enormous power were responsible for crucial changes to our planet.

parasite

Who would want to be a **parasite**? In Ancient Greece, lots of people did. The word literally meant "beside" (*para*) "food" (*sitos*).

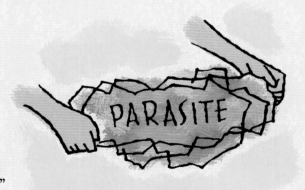

At first, a parasite was religious: somebody who helped a high priest in temple rituals. Then the word moved from the temple to the dining room. If you hung around a rich man, making flattering comments in a witty manner, you might get invited home to dinner—a much better dinner than you could afford to buy. Greek writers would often put parasites into their plays, just as writers for today's sitcoms like to find a place for smart alecks. Then the Romans, who borrowed so much from Greek theater, imported the word into Latin. In their writings, too, a *parasitus* made his living by amusing the rich. Roman authors found the *parasitus* a useful target for satire and a good way of pointing out the corruption in society.

Like catastrophe, parasite was hauled into English in the middle of the 16th century. At first, it meant a hanger-on: somebody who depended on others. But in 1646, when the scientific method as we know it was taking shape, the word got its big break. It began to mean a plant or animal that lives off its host. Without a host, the parasite starves.

We can still use the term to refer to a person—if you take unfair advantage of someone else, giving little or nothing in return, you risk being called a parasite. That meaning is not too far from the Greek and Latin sense. But we think of this as the metaphorical meaning, not the chief one. For us, the dominant meaning of parasite is the scientific usage: a small organism like a tapeworm or flea that feeds on the larger organism that gives it life. Ancient Greek priests would be astonished.

telephone

The Greeks who lived 2,500 years ago were familiar with catastrophes, parasites, and fantasies—but they never saw a **telephone**. The device was invented in the 19ᵗʰ century. Who deserves the lion's share of credit? That's fiercely disputed among Italians, French, Germans, Scots, Canadians, and Americans. Yet the word is pure Greek. *Tele* means "far"; *phone* means "sound" or "voice." Announcing his discovery—or, some would say, his clever adaptation—in 1876, Alexander Graham Bell wrote: "I placed the membrane of the telephone near my mouth."

A simple word? Not really. We remember the great scientific advances of the 19ᵗʰ century, but we seldom think of the many false starts and dead ends. As a word—though not as a working device for long-distance conversation—telephone had been around for nearly half a century before Bell's triumphant moment, and it had meant several things.

At first, it referred to a system of electric signals that sent out musical notes. Then it came to mean a device that transmitted loud noises in one direction only.

One version of a telephone resembled a foghorn. A French inventor used the word to describe a way of transmitting speech through iron pipes, filled with water and laid below ground. And a German scientist invented what he called *das Telephon*: a magnetic device with a microphone that could transmit continuous musical tones. Finally, the telephone as we know it made all these earlier meanings irrelevant.

Even before Bell's first memorable exchange with his assistant, Thomas Watson, telephone was an internationally accepted word. The French probably used it first, but (with slight variations of spelling) it quickly became a part of German, Italian, Spanish, and many other tongues. Most European languages share a Latin and Greek heritage, and this makes it natural for Latin and Greek roots to be used when fresh words are needed. **Hypertext**, which combines a Greek adjective and a Latin noun, is an example from the world of computers. If you talk about a **cell** or a **mobile**, you're substituting a Latin word for a Greek one.

To: Dad & Mom
From: Alex Boswell
Sent: July 26
Subject: the wastelands
. . . .

Dear Mom and Dad,

Today was our last field trip. A weird one! Tomorrow we'll pack our bags, clean up the camp, and start saying our goodbyes. Noah says if I write down all the stuff I learned in the last couple of days, I'll remember it better in the future. So here goes.

We had a rest day yesterday, and Dr. Murray gave an optional talk in the afternoon on the history of ancient languages. Not many campers went, and I was surprised to see Andreas and Jill there. Dr. M said it would be "splendid preparation" for today's field trip into the Indo-European Wastelands.

You see, I've been wrong about something. I thought that the farther we moved from camp in the last week or so, the deeper we'd been going into the history of English. But that isn't totally right. Dr. M said that many of the Greek and Latin fossils we've found are a few hundred years old—not a few thousand years old. They come from the Renaissance, when people were hungry to expand the language. In our final days at camp, he wants us to glimpse some of the really old stuff that lies behind Old English and Old Norse—to get down to the deepest layers of language we can reach.

Dr. M talked about Gothic, and he said it had nothing to do with reading scary novels or wearing heavy makeup and black clothes. It turns out that Gothic was a Germanic language, same as Old English and Old Norse. In fact, it was the earliest Germanic language to be written down, roughly 1,700 years ago. Even though it's been extinct for centuries, we know quite a bit about it. Dr. M does, anyway. He said only a few English words come from Gothic—**heathen** probably comes from the Gothic *haithi*, meaning "living in an open field." But Gothic leads us toward the heart of Proto-Germanic.

When Dr. M was talking about Proto-Germanic, I have to admit my attention wandered a bit. But I did catch that *proto* means "first" or "original." Basically, this is the ancestor of all the Germanic languages, but it was never written down so it's kind of mysterious.

I was daydreaming about our new home and our old one when Andreas put up his hand and said, "So when you move that far back in history, is etymology just a guessing game?" I don't think Dr. Murray liked the question because he hemmed and hawed for a while, and his Scottish accent got more obvious. He said there are lots of technical points that linguists understand, like how vowels shift over time and how verb tenses are clumped in patterns, and these technical points make it less of a guessing game than Andreas imagined. But he didn't really say "no."

Then he moved on to something I found more interesting: Sanskrit, the mother language of India. Or maybe I should say "grandmother language"? More than a billion people live in India, and an awful lot of them speak languages that grew out of Sanskrit: Hindi, Urdu, Bengali, and a bunch of others. You might say that what Latin is to European languages, Sanskrit is to Indian languages. It's just about dead now, same as Latin. For a long time, nobody realized that Sanskrit was related to English because it looked so different. Dr. M gave us a sheet of paper with a sentence on it: *agrāhyā mūrdhajeṣv etā striyo guṇasamanvitāh*. Do you recognize anything there? I sure didn't. (Dr. M translated it as "Ladies like these, who are accomplished, should not be seized by the hair." I heard Jill snort loudly.)

But if you know how to see it, there *is* a relationship to English because Sanskrit and all those Indian languages I mentioned belong to the huge Indo-European family, just like English and French and Latin and Greek. Dr. M gave us all a sheet for our binder with some information about Sir William Jones, the first guy to understand the link. Back in the 1700s, he realized that Greek, Latin, and Sanskrit have a strong resemblance in their verbs and grammar that couldn't possibly be the result of accident—they must have "sprung from some common source, which, perhaps, no longer exists." Get rid of the "perhaps": he was talking about Proto-Indo-European.

So Sanskrit is not our ancestor; Sanskrit is more like an amazing old cousin in a sari. Sanskrit and English share the same ancestor, or maybe I should say Sanskrit and Proto-Germanic and Greek and all the Romance languages share the same ancestor, which people spoke maybe 6,000 years ago. In fact, about half the people alive in the world today speak languages that are descended from Proto-Indo-European. That's what we were trying to discover on our field trip today: our Proto-Indo-European roots.

But honestly, I don't know if it was such a great idea. On our earlier trips, the fossils seemed like they were waiting for us to dig them up. On this one, it was like they wanted to keep their secrets. The Indo-European landscape was kind of creepy—even the light was different. Instead of being dry and sharp like it normally is in the badlands, it felt murky. Low clouds and fog patches kept hanging around, and when we passed a swamp, the mosquitoes were demonic. The counselors had to work hard to keep everyone together—it would have been easy to get lost. At one point, I stayed behind the rest of the group because I thought I'd found a fossil. But the more I looked at it, the less sure I was—and then I realized the others had all gone on ahead and I couldn't see anyone. My heart was racing till I caught up.

I'm sure there were words all around, but it was like they hadn't formed into well-defined shapes—they were more like ghosts. Dr. Murray calls this area the Indo-European Wastelands, but I think he could also call them the Indo-European Waitlands. Imagine all the future words just waiting to take shape.

How strange was it out there? Well, Keshia didn't find a single fossil. Our entire group only discovered four or five, but I think we must have walked past dozens of others, or even hundreds. The one I remember best is a rock I actually picked up. Except I didn't realize it was a fossil—Daniel was the one who said, "Hey, man!" Noah and a couple of the other counselors decided the word would have sounded like *wed* in Proto-Indo-European. That's where we get our **water**, and it's also where the Russians get their *voda* and the Greeks their *hydōr*. (Andreas seemed pretty happy about that.) All these words go back to *wed*.

The mood was kind of meh on our way back. I overheard one of the counselors say, "Well, what can you expect from a language we know almost nothing about?"

When we got back to camp, I tried looking for Jill but I couldn't find her. Tomorrow, I'll talk to her about the trip home.

See you soon!

Alex

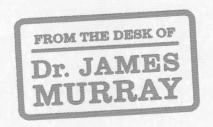
Two words from Proto-Indo-European

equestrian

For centuries after Sir
William Jones proposed
the existence of Proto-
Indo-European, debate
raged about where
its speakers lived.
Eastern Europe, Turkey,
and central Asia were
among the candidates. The
Mediterranean can be ruled out because
Proto-Indo-European lacked words for "ship" and "ocean."
But in recent years, scholars have just about settled the
debate. We can now be reasonably sure that the Indo-
European homeland lay in the flat plains northeast of the
Black Sea. Today that area belongs to Ukraine and Russia.

The people who lived there about 6,000 years ago
succeeded in spreading their language far and wide. Why?
Not because their words were better than any other
words of the time, but because they were the first to

master horse riding. The new ability gave the riders a tremendous edge over their neighbors and rivals. Not only did it make long-distance travel much easier than it is on foot, it also changed the nature of war.

A key word in their language must have been the term for **horse**—so we'd expect related words to show up in many Indo-European languages. As they do. For example, the Latin term is *equus*—the origin of **equestrian**, an English word that means "relating to horseback riding." The Irish word is *ech*. And so on. Even the Sanskrit word *ašvah*, although it looks very different, has the same source: a word that horse riders and chariot drivers across the flatlands of Ukraine uttered 6,000 years ago.

Linguists believe the word for horse is *ekwos*. But they put an asterisk in front of this and all other words in Proto-Indo-European because they have no way of proving the point. The asterisk shows that the word is merely guesswork. Trying to reconstruct the language is like trying to reconstruct the walls and roof of a building on the basis of impressions left in the ground. Proto-Indo-European was never written down; its speakers were illiterate. But that doesn't mean the language was primitive. Its grammar is thought to have been quite complex.

So why do English speakers use a word that has no direct relation to *ekwos*? Horse is a Germanic word, and all Germanic languages belong to the huge Indo-European family. Again, linguists are not certain. Their best guess is that horses were sacred to the early Germanic tribes, who built up a strong religious taboo against uttering their original name. Rather than pronounce a magical word like *ekwos,* they invented a new word of their own.

axle

Like pigs, sheep, cattle, and goats—all of which had been tamed much earlier—horses at first served as a source of meat. Centuries after they began to use horses as food, the early Indo-Europeans realized they could also ride them. Later still, they understood how to make carts with solid wheels, which the horses could pull. That knowledge of the wheel gave the Indo-Europeans a big advantage in food production as well as warfare.

One of the crucial steps in all this was their invention of the **axle**—the central bar or shaft of a rotating wheel. Without the use of a weight-bearing axle, wheels would be unable to keep their proper position. They would spin out of control. Linguists can't be confident about many words in Proto-Indo-European, but for humble concepts like **wheel**, **axle**, **oxen**, **plough**, and **yoke**, they have few doubts.

The Proto-Indo-European term for axle, *aks,* is the source of the word for axle in many languages, such as *ýxull* in Icelandic, *eixo* in Portuguese, *axon* in Greek, and *aksah* in Sanskrit. In Latin, it became *axis,* a word that also entered English. An **axis** has many scientific meanings, such as the imaginary line around which Earth rotates, the main stem of a plant, a reference line from which angles are measured, and a bone in the neck.

So whenever a geographer, a botanist, a mathematician, or a medical doctor speaks about an axis, he or she is using a word that goes straight back to the wheel shafts of Proto-Indo-European.

To: Michael Boswell, Karen Boswell

cc: Kelly Monahan

From: Murray, Dr. James A.

Sent: July 26

Subject: Troubling news

· ·

Dear Mr. and Mrs. Boswell,

I am sending you this e-mail at an extremely late hour, having tried
and failed to reach you by telephone. As the director of Camp Fossil
Eyes, I have the unpleasant duty of telling you some troubling
news. Your daughter, Jillian, did not return to camp today from
her field trip to the Indo-European Wastelands. Strictly speaking,
they are not wastelands, of course; that is our metaphorical way of
expressing how little we know about the long-dead language that is
the ultimate source of everything from English and French to Latin,
Greek, and Sanskrit. But its paths are little traveled, so to speak.
I must add that your son, Alexander, is safe and sound.

It appears that Jillian and one of her friends split off from the main
party as they were exploring the wastelands earlier today, and
although they assured the group that they would eventually reunite
with them, they failed to do so. It was Jillian's counselor, Kelly
Monahan, who noticed that the two young people were missing,
and she has stayed behind in the wastelands, along with a fellow
counselor. I have every confidence that they will find the young
people soon. If they are not successful tonight, we will send out a
full search party in the morning.

I realize this news will come as a great shock to you both, and I assure you that we will keep you informed as soon as there are new developments. Please accept my apologies and my deepest concern.

Sincerely yours,

J. A. Murray

To: Karen and Michael Boswell
cc: Dr. J. A. Murray
From: Kelly Monahan
Sent: July 27
Subject: Jill

. . . .

Dear Mr. and Mrs. Boswell,

Kelly Monahan here. It's 2:00 a.m. and I just got back to camp.
I gather Dr. Murray has told you the bad news. Before I go to bed
and try to grab a few hours' sleep, I wanted to send you a quick
e-mail and explain what happened.

Jill and Andreas were very excited to be on the trip—such a contrast
from Jill's first days at Camp Fossil Eyes! They began to explore the
strange landscape of Proto-Indo-European as soon as we arrived.
But perhaps we counselors hadn't made it clear enough that this
region is not like the Greek Mountains, the Latin Alps, or any of the
other prominent formations in these badlands. It's relatively easy
to find your way around those areas, and they contain well-defined
fossils. With Proto-Indo-European, nothing is clear. Everything is
guesswork. The trails begin clearly enough, but soon peter out. You
may think you've found a pattern in a rock, but when you turn it over
and look at it closely, you wonder if you're imagining things.

Not surprisingly, most of the campers found Proto-Indo-European
somewhat frustrating to tackle. But Jill and Andreas kept their
enthusiasm and wanted to go even deeper into the wastelands.
I remember pointing out the shaggy mass of Proto-World lurking

in the far distance—way beyond Indo-European and every other language group we know of—it's what the earliest humans might have spoken, tens of thousands of years ago. Many linguists believe that Proto-World can never really be known. But Jill's eyes lit up and she said it would be cool to explore. I should have guessed, given her impulsive nature, that she and Andreas intended to do this right away. But I had other campers to look after, and a few of them were getting discouraged. Only at the end of the afternoon did I realize Jill and her boyfriend were missing.

I feel absolutely terrible about this, and I apologize from the bottom of my heart. Despite their ominous name, the wastelands are not hugely dangerous—I would be even more worried if Jill was lost on a high mountain. The Indo-European terrain is confusing, but it shouldn't be physically treacherous.  She and Andreas are fairly well equipped—they had some food and water with them—and the night is dry. I asked Dr. Murray about rattlesnakes, and he said they are very uncommon in that part of the badlands. There may be a few coyotes around, but surely they wouldn't attack a couple of teenagers.

We *will* find Jill and Andreas later today, I'm certain, and I'll write to you again as soon as we do—

Kelly

To: Dad & Mom
From: Alex Boswell
Sent: July 27
Subject: Found

· ·

Mom, Dad,

Jill is safe. Andreas, too. They were found a couple of hours ago, wandering around in the wastelands. They're hungry and tired and stuff, but they're okay.

Hugs from

Alex

To: Karen and Michael Boswell
From: Kelly Monahan
Sent: July 27
Subject: Jill is fine

. . . .

Hi Mr. and Mrs. Boswell,

I know you've spoken to Dr.
Murray by telephone, so
you've heard the fantastic
news. I'm so relieved, I
can't tell you. Jill is in
good shape, considering
the ordeal she has gone
through. The camp nurse
has checked her over and
she seems to be fine. She's
even cracking the occasional joke.

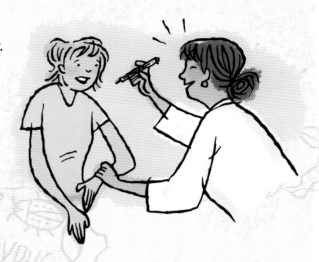

We went back to the Indo-European Wastelands at first light this
morning—myself and most of the other counselors. I remembered
the spot where I'd last seen Jill and Andreas, and that's where we
headed first. But we couldn't find any trace of them, so we moved
deeper into the area, toward the distant mass of Proto-World. The
land is strangely featureless—I admit I found it a little eerie—and we
kept whistling and shouting.

After we'd been walking for about an hour, Noah Steiner noticed
some footprints along the edge of a muddy stream. The footprints

soon disappeared, but we fanned out and within a few minutes I caught sight of Jill and Andreas standing beside a dead tree, uncertain where to go next. I yelled at them and they were obviously very, very happy to be found. We gave them water and dark chocolate right away—they'd exhausted their supplies.

Andreas said it was all his fault. He had encouraged Jill to head off with him because he wanted to see what they could discover about Proto-World. He knew that **finger** in Greek is *daktilos,* and he'd heard that many other languages have a similar word. He's right—the root for "finger" in a pair of African language groups is *tok* and *tak*, and in the Indo-Pacific group, it's *dik*, and so on. Our word **digit** is related. But how far you can go with this, nobody really knows, and it was crazy of Andreas to think he might be able to produce an answer. Crazy, though maybe also typical.

Jill says she will e-mail you in the next few hours, after she's had a chance to rest. She will be flying home tomorrow, and while I'm very sad that her camp experience has ended in such an alarming way, I hope she'll be able to look back on these weeks with some pleasure. I know she has learned a huge amount.

Best wishes,

Kelly

To: parents
From: Jillian Boswell
Sent: July 27
Subject: Leaving Fossil Eyes

. . . .

My dear mother and father,

Honestly, I don't know what to say.

I'm sorry to have caused so much trouble, I didn't mean to sabotage the last days of camp, I'm exhausted because we hardly got any sleep last night, I'm happy that Kelly found us—she's an awesome lady, did I ever tell you?—and you'll probably hate me for saying this, but I'm also really sad to be leaving Camp Fossil Eyes.

Andreas is not a terrible person. He didn't—what's that phrase of yours, Mother?—he didn't try to take any liberties. Don't go berserk, please. Don't think badly of him. What happened to us was not a catastrophe. Not in the modern sense, anyway.

His parents wouldn't allow him to stay on in August, so he's leaving tomorrow, too. But he really cares about language—in fact, he wants to be an etymologist. He's determined to come here again and find out about all the words we didn't get enough of a chance to explore this summer—African American, and Italian, and Japanese, and German, and so on. It's endless, the discoveries we can make.

So can I please come back next summer? Please?

Love,

Jill

To: Dad & Mom
From: Alex Boswell
Sent: July 28
Subject: Fast hi

. . . .

The plane is a few minutes late, so I'm sending you a quick message from a terminal in the departure lounge. Just wanted to tell you we're on our way. Jill is okay—not saying much, but I expect she'll talk to me in a while. Or not.

A new home, wow. Before I left Camp Fossil Eyes, Noah gave me one last sheet for my binder. I'm looking at it now—bet you didn't know that **home** goes back more than 1,000 years and is related to the Gothic word for village, *heims*. It also has links to our word **haunt**, which may come from the Old Norse *heimta* (to lead home). But then somehow a French word—

Oops, my time is up!

Glossary

Algonquian languages: A family of more than 20 languages spoken across much of northern Canada and parts of the United States. Among the best-known Algonquian languages are Cree, Blackfoot, Ojibwa, and Cheyenne.

Ancient Greek: The language of Greece about 2,500 years ago. It evolved gradually into Modern Greek. Along with Latin, it was crucial to the development of European culture.

Dark Ages: An old term for the period after the fall of the Roman Empire in AD 476, lasting four or five centuries. Most people now say Early Middle Ages instead.

Endangered language: A language that is at risk of dying out within the next few years, usually because it's spoken only by older people. Their children and grandchildren have switched over to English, Chinese, Russian, or some other widely used language.

Etymologist: A person who studies the origin and history of words.

False splitting: A process by which, over a long period of time, a word changes its shape after being heard wrongly by many people. For example, a *napron* (Middle English) gradually became an apron (Modern English).

Germanic language: One of a group of European languages that includes not only German but also English, Dutch, and the Nordic tongues. They share a common ancestor, Proto-Germanic, that was spoken in northern Europe a few thousand years ago.

Gothic: An extinct Germanic language spoken more than 1,000 years ago in parts of Europe.

Grammar: The set of rules that governs how a language is used, including word order, verb tenses, plural forms, and so on. Unrelated languages (like English and Japanese) have very different grammars. Related languages (like English and French) have similarities in their grammar.

Indigenous language: A language used by the original residents of a place, before invaders or colonists arrived there. For example, Cree is the indigenous language spoken across much of northern Canada. Many indigenous languages are now endangered.

Indo-European: A very important family of languages, stretching all the way from Iceland in the west to Bangladesh in the east—before spreading even farther, through conquest and settlement, to become dominant in the Americas and Australia. English, Spanish, Russian, German, and French are among the hundreds of Indo-European languages.

Latin: The language of the Roman Empire. It already existed by 600 BCE and survived as a spoken language in Europe until about AD 1000. For centuries after that, it continued to be used by priests, diplomats, and scholars around the world. Indeed, it is still taught in a few schools today.

Linguist: In the past, the word meant a person who could speak many languages; today, it means someone who studies language in a scientific way. A linguist might examine how sounds are made, how grammar is organized, how the mind uses words, and so on.

Literal meaning: The exact, word-by-word meaning of a phrase. Sometimes it may not make a lot of sense, as in "he's gone off his head."

Metaphorical meaning: What the words of a phrase are intended to suggest. The metaphorical meaning of "he's gone off his head" is "he's gone crazy."

Middle Ages: A long period in European history. It does not have precise boundaries, but often it refers to the time between the end of the Roman Empire and the Renaissance—nearly 1,000 years.

Middle English: The form of English that was spoken between about 1100 and 1450, late in the Middle Ages, and that featured the arrival of many French words. It was followed by Early Modern English (1450–1650).

Modern English: The form of English that has been spoken since about 1650. Although it has changed a lot over that period, it remains recognizably the same language.

Nenets: A language spoken in a remote part of northern Russia. It belongs to the Uralic family. In the area where it's used, Russian is the language of education, and children often speak Russian in their homes. As a result, Nenets is at risk of becoming an endangered language.

Nordic language: Any one of several languages descended from Old Norse. Examples are Norwegian, Danish, Swedish, and Icelandic. This group is also called North Germanic.

Old English: The ancient language that slowly developed into what we speak today. Tribes from the continent of Europe crossed the sea and brought their way of speaking to England before AD 500. Old English (also known as Anglo-Saxon) lasted until about 1100.

Old Norse: The language spoken by the Vikings between about AD 800 and 1300.

Portmanteau word: A word made up by combining bits of other words. For example, "brunch" is made up of the first two letters of "breakfast" and the last four of "lunch."

Proto-Indo-European: The language that was presumably spoken by the common ancestor of all the Indo-European peoples, more than 7,000 years ago. This was the source from which English, Latin, Greek, and all the other Indo-European languages emerged—a source we know very little about because it was never written down.

Proto-World: Some linguists say that all human speech emerged from a single source. If they are right, that source was Proto-World: the first of all human languages, probably spoken more than 50,000 years ago. Nobody knows how it would have sounded.

Renaissance: The cultural and artistic movement that launched the modern world. It began in Italy around 1300 and spread throughout Europe. The word is a French term meaning "rebirth"—because during the Renaissance, people rediscovered Latin and Greek texts that had been forgotten during the Middle Ages.

Romance language: Any one of a group of European languages that emerged out of Latin after the fall of the Roman Empire. The four best-known Romance languages are French, Spanish, Portuguese, and Italian.

Sanskrit: An ancient and complex language spoken for many centuries in India. Like Latin, which is its European equivalent, Sanskrit lies at the root of various languages that are commonly heard today.

Synonym: A word with a very similar meaning to another word. "Small" and "little" are synonyms; "small" and "large" are antonyms.

Uralic family: A family of about 40 languages, spoken in parts of eastern Europe and northern Asia. The best known are Hungarian and Finnish.

Further Reading

Baker, Rosalie, and Tom Lopes. *In a Word: 750 Words and Their Fascinating Stories and Origins*. Chicago: Cricket Books, 2003.

O'Reilly, Gillian, and Krista Johnson. *Slangalicious: Where We Got That Crazy Lingo*. Vancouver and Toronto: Annick Press, 2004.

Terban, Marvin, and Giulio Maestro. *Guppies in Tuxedos: Funny Eponyms*. New York: Sandpiper, 2008.

Umstatter, Jack. *Where Words Come From*. Danbury, CT: Children's Press, 2003.

For Older Readers

Abley, Mark. *The Prodigal Tongue: Dispatches From the Future of English*. Toronto: Random House Canada, 2008.

Austin, Peter K. *One Thousand Languages: Living, Endangered, and Lost*. Berkeley and Los Angeles: University of California Press, 2008.

Blount, Roy, Jr. *Alphabet Juice: The Energies, Gists, and Spirits of Letters, Words, and Combinations Thereof: Their Roots, Bones, Innards, Piths, Pips, and Secret Parts, Tinctures, Tonics, and Essences; With Examples of Their Usage Foul and Savory*. New York: Farrar, Straus and Giroux, 2008.

Crystal, David. *The Stories of English*. London: Penguin Books, 2004.

Essinger, James. *Spellbound: The Surprising Origins and Astonishing Secrets of English Spelling*. London: Robson Books, 2006.

Hitchings, Henry. *The Secret Life of Words: How English Became English*. London: John Murray, 2008.

Hole, Georgia. *The Real McCoy: The True Stories Behind Our Everyday Phrases*. Oxford: Oxford University Press, 2005.

Nadeau, Jean-Benoît, and Julie Barlow. *The Story of French*. Toronto: Alfred A. Knopf Canada, 2006.

Ostler, Nicholas. *Ad Infinitum: A Biography of Latin*. New York: Walker and Company, 2007.

Robinson, Andrew. *Lost Languages: The Enigma of the World's Undeciphered Scripts*. New York: McGraw-Hill, 2002.

West, Paul. *The Secret Life of Words*. New York: Harcourt, 2000.

Winchester, Simon. *The Meaning of Everything: The Story of the Oxford English Dictionary*. Oxford: Oxford University Press, 2003.

Selected Sources

Anthony, David W. *The Horse, the Wheel, and Language: How Bronze-Age Riders From the Eurasian Steppes Shaped the Modern World.* Princeton: Princeton University Press, 2007.

Ayto, John. *Twentieth Century Words: The Story of the New Words in English Over the Last Hundred Years.* Oxford: Oxford University Press, 1999.

Carver, Craig M. *A History of English in Its Own Words.* New York: Harper Collins, 1991.

Hodgson, Charles. *Carnal Knowledge: A Navel Gazer's Dictionary of Anatomy, Etymology, and Trivia.* New York: St. Martin's Press, 2007.

Macrone, Michael. *It's Greek to Me: Brush Up Your Classics.* New York: Harper Collins, 1991.

Metcalf, Allan. *The World in So Many Words: A Country-by-Country Tour of Words That Have Shaped Our Language.* Boston and New York: Houghton Mifflin, 1999.

Oxford English Dictionary, 2nd ed. Oxford: Oxford University Press, 1989.

Quinion, Michael. *Port Out, Starboard Home: And Other Language Myths.* London: Penguin Books, 2004.

Steinmetz, Sol. *Semantic Antics: How and Why Words Change Meaning.* New York: Random House, 2008.

Index

abominable snowman, 60
Aboriginals (Australia), 19–21
accent, 31–32, 61
African words, 30–31
Aleuts, 71
Alexander, meaning of, 93–94
Algonquian, 18–19, 120
American English, 17–18, 61, 89
anger, 64
Angles, 39–40, 42
Anglo-Saxon. *See* Old English
ankle, 38
appendix, 77–78
Arabic, 30–31, 72
axis, 109
axle, 108–9

bad, 61
badlands, 2, 8, 60–61
bafflegab, 82
Bell, Alexander Graham, 98
Beowulf, 40
berserk, 66–67
bi-, 58
bikini, 57–58
boomerang, 19–21
booze, 74
broadcast, 27
buccaneer, 14–15
bug, 47

catastrophe, 95–96
chatroom, 45
chatter, 45

Chaucer, Geoffrey, 68
checkmate, 84–85
Chicago, 19
chipmunk, 11
chocolate, 16
Clarke, Arthur C., 26
cookie, 74

dadrock, 24
Daniel, meaning of, 94
Dark Ages, 80, 120
demon, 91
Dharuk, 20
digit, 116
Dutch, 72–74, 120

Early Middle English, 42, 51
Early Modern English, 43, 122
egg, 65
Emerson, Ralph Waldo, 8
endangered languages, 29, 120–21
equestrian, 107–8
etymologist, 3, 102, 120

face, 80
face-off, 81
false splitting, 55, 120
fantastic, 92
fossils, words as, 7–8, 53, 62
French, 14, 17, 50–58, 61, 63, 66, 73, 83, 87, 99, 121, 124

German, 99, 120
Germanic languages, 51, 101, 107, 120

gorilla, 91–92
gossip, 44–45
Gothic, 101, 121
grammar, 103, 121
Greek, 72–73, 90–99, 100, 103, 109, 116, 120
Gullah, 30

heathen, 101
Hebrew, 94
hippies, 24
hipster, 24–25
home, 119
horse, 107–8
hypertext, 99

Icelandic, 66, 109, 122
indigenous languages, 10–21, 61, 71, 92, 121
Indo-European languages, 103, 107–8, 110, 121
inter-, 81
interface, 80–82
Internet, 81
invention of words, 26–27, 29
Italian, 52, 99, 124

Jillian, meaning of, 78
Jones, Sir William, 103, 106

Kumbaya, 30

lady, 46–47
ladybug, 45–47
land, 61
language academies, 71

language changes, 61–62, 89
Latin, 51–52, 66, 73, 76–83, 90, 95, 97, 99, 100, 102, 107, 109, 121
linguist, 102, 107–8, 121
literal meaning, 122

maneuver, 83
manure, 82–83
Marshallese, 58
McLuhan, Marshall, 82
meh, 28
metaphorical meaning, 21, 122
Middle English, 42–44, 51–52, 54, 68, 120, 122
Modern English, 31, 47, 52, 120, 122
mongrel languages, 31, 52
mosquito, 86

Nahuatl, 16
Narragansett, 18
Nenets, 70–71, 122
new words, 23–29
nice, 51
nickname, 55
Nordic languages, 66, 120, 122

Ojibwa, 11, 18, 120
Old English, 35–46, 51–52, 68, 100–1, 123
Old Norse, 38, 63–68, 73, 100–1, 123

papoose, 18
paradise, 85
parasite, 96–97
parka, 70–71
Persian, 84–85

pickle, 74–75
podcast, 26–27
portmanteau words, 27, 123
Portuguese, 14, 52, 109, 124
propaganda, 79–80
proto-, 102
Proto-Germanic, 101–3, 120
Proto-Indo-European, 103–5, 106–110, 112, 123
Proto-World, 112-13, 115–16, 123

quahog, 18

ranch, 87–88
Renaissance, 80, 82, 95, 100, 123
rock, 24
Roman Catholicism, 77, 80
Romance languages, 52, 66, 103, 124
Roman Empire, 52, 77, 79–80, 121

sabotage, 55–56
saboteur, 56
salary, 62
Salish, 15
Sanskrit, 102–3, 107, 109, 124
sarcasm, 90–91
Saxons, 40, 42
Scott, Sir Walter, 67
Shakespeare, William, 43
Shelley, Percy, 43
sibling, 44
Simpsons, The, 28
sky, 67–68
sockeye, 15
Spanish, 52, 86–89, 99, 124
squash, 17–18

synonym, 124

Taino, 15
tankini, 58
telephone, 98–99
television, 90
ten gallon, 87
Tibetan, 60
Tupí, 14

ugly, 65
umpire, 54–55
universe, 76
Uralic languages, 71, 122, 124

Vikings, 63, 66–67

water, 105
weird, 35, 42–43
weirdo, 43
welkin, 68

Yiddish, 28

About the Author

Mark Abley spent part of his childhood in southern Alberta, which is famous for its badlands. He grew up to be a Rhodes Scholar and a Guggenheim Fellow. Now the father of two daughters, he lives with his family in Montreal. He is the author or editor of a dozen books, including *Spoken Here: Travels Among Threatened Languages* and *The Prodigal Tongue: Dispatches From the Future of English.*

About the Illustrator

Kathryn Adams is an illustrator who lives in Toronto. She is also an educator at Sheridan College and the Ontario College of Art and Design, where she teaches business skills to aspiring illustrators. Kathryn has been illustrating for 22 years and has received awards from *American Illustration*, *3x3*, *Applied Arts*, and the Art Directors Club of Canada.